GLASS STORIES

IVY GRIMES

GLASS STORIES

IVY GRIMES

New Orleans, Louisiana

© 2024 Grimscribe Press
Cover art by Jesse Peper

All rights reserved. No part of this publication may be reproduced, distributed, or transmitted in any form or by any means, including photocopying, recording, or other electronic or mechanical methods, without the prior written permission of the publisher, except in the case of brief quotations embodied in critical reviews and certain other noncommercial uses permitted by copyright law.
Published by

Grimscribe Press
New Orleans, LA
USA

grimscribepress.com

CONTENTS

GLASS TOWER	5
GLASS MOTHER	11
GLASS BOOK	21
GLASS CLUE	29
GLASS TURTLE	39
GLASS ART	51
GLASS COFFINS	59
GLASS MUSEUM	71
GLASS ANGEL	79
LOOKING GLASS	87
GLASS PET	95
GLASS PIANO	101
GLASS MOUNTAIN	105
GLASS PILLS	111
GLASS CABBAGE	115
GLASS HOUSE	121
GLASS APPLE	123

Glass Tower

THE OLD WOMAN saw a shadow through the wall. The glass was frosted and glowed with a bit of blue light, so she could only make out shapes and shades of what was outside.

"Come in!" she called to the shadow. She always invited them in, though most ran away.

This shadow grew larger, then touched the glass wall with a hand.

"Come in!"

The shadow swayed, as if dancing.

"There's an entryway to your left!"

To the old woman's surprise, the shadow went left and found the recessed opening. Stumbling, the shadow crept through the winding entry until the old woman found herself in the presence of a young woman.

"Sorry. I was lost." The young woman wore a shirt that was too small and a blanket draped around her waist to look like a skirt.

"Lost from where?"

"I was asked to leave my house."

"Why?" The old woman stood up from her glass chair and stirred the fire in her glass stove. The girl had probably noticed the smoke in the distance. It took a good observer to see the smoke and the blue glow of the house, but she didn't want to compliment the girl right away.

"This looks like a castle of ice." The girl's voice was tinny and weak, like she was trying to speak through a heavy door.

"I made it."

"How?"

"I asked for it," the old woman said.

"It rises so high in the air. Maybe five, seven stories. Maybe more. Do you ever go up there?"

"Why were you turned out of your house?" the old woman said. This girl was bolder than most visitors. She must have been hungry. The old woman urged her to have a seat in front of the fire and handed her a mug of broth and a bowl of ice cream.

The girl seemed disgusted by the food.

"What do you eat?"

"What I find out there. Pecans and chestnuts. Pears. Mushrooms. White roots."

She took away the mug and bowl and handed the girl an apple.

"It's like a pear, except crisper."

The sound of teeth in the apple was like the soles of the old woman's shoes on the glass floor. When the old woman had asked for the glass house, she'd thought it would be refreshing.

"Did you ever ask for anything else?" the girl said.

The old woman found some old blankets on her glass shelves, and she made the girl sit on them while she returned to her glass chair. It was hard and cold, but it was what she liked.

"Before I received this glass place, I received many other things from the one who listens," the old woman said.

"Good things?"

"I didn't ask for good things."

"Why?"

"I was bored. Or I didn't know what good things were."

"This apple is good," the girl said in a friendly way.

The old woman smiled to be polite, but she asked again. "Who made you leave your home?"

The girl shivered. "It was my landlord."

"You're young to have a landlord."

"He said the house was full, and he needed my room. A family of four needed to live there."

"You could have asked to share a room with another tenant."

"It was all so full. Except for the basement, and I couldn't stand that place. I went there once, and it was so…" She took another bite of her apple.

Her hair was cut short. She must have had a pair of scissors at least. And she was clean.

"You bathe in the river," the old woman said.

"I live beside the river. It's the best place."

"No doubt."

"I was scared at first."

"Why?"

"To be out of doors, away from my…"

"Your family?"

"Yes."

"Why did they let the landlord get rid of you?"

She looked at her blanket-skirt. She had done all right for herself, whatever had happened.

"I never had a landlord. I don't know why I said that."

"That's okay. I'm asking hard questions. There's nothing pleasant or normal to talk about out here."

"My stepmother got rid of me after watching a show about owls. She said we all have to fly away eventually. Started worrying she'd stunted my development."

The old woman had seen that show. She could watch whatever she wanted on a screen of glass. If she wanted, the blue glow would change itself into stories, and she could see patterns. But the show about owls shouldn't have caused the stepmother to ask the girl to leave her house.

The girl continued. "The point is that people are like animals. When my father was alive, he said we should eat him in case of a famine. He said we should get him drunk and hit him over the head. He was our savior. I couldn't eat him, so my stepmother gave me the last of the bread, and she ate him. That way, we lived until it rained. Together. We chose a stuffed animal and named him after my father. When we were in trouble, we prayed to him. You don't forget a sacrifice like that in a lifetime."

"You can stay here as long as you like," the old woman said. "There are other floors, and other people live there. I said they could stay. They won't harm you."

The girl put her half-eaten apple on the glass floor. It was hard to tell what she wanted. She didn't seem to like the idea of other people. Maybe she thought she'd be happier in her own house of glass.

"She was my mother, not my stepmother. I don't know why I said that. I guess I thought it made the story better. All you are to other people is a story. Maybe a funny story, and maybe a sad one. It really doesn't matter as long as they want to know about you," the girl said.

A storm outside whipped against the glass, and lightning brightened the night. A crack of thunder sounded like it would split the glass. The girl hugged herself.

"No need to fear," the old woman said.

"I was alone for so long in the woods," the girl said. "I couldn't see anything but stars and branches and the little pebbly gaze of the moon. When I saw the blue glow in the distance, it hurt at first. I didn't want to remember what it was to live near someone else."

"You ate your mother," the old woman said.

The girl looked up at her with wide eyes. "How did you know? You must be a witch."

"Everyone who's alive had to eat someone to stay that way. Except for me. I asked for my glass house to always be filled with food."

"You are lucky."

The old woman shifted in her chair and felt uncomfortable for a change. "I have the decency to feel guilty about it, at least."

A darkness washed over them. When the old woman looked up, she saw another shadow outside. The shadow was trying to find the entry, but no one could unless the old woman told them where it was.

"The opening is to your right!" she shouted.

The girl cowered and drew closer to the old woman. "What if this is a monster? Or an enemy?"

The shadow disappeared, and a middle-aged woman found her way inside the glass house. She looked in awe at the glass kitchen.

"It's so warm in here," the woman said.

The old woman whispered to the girl. "She can be your new mother."

The girl looked uncertain.

"You can call her your stepmother if you want."

That seemed to comfort the girl. The old woman gave the woman and the girl a stack of blankets and sent them up the stairs to the room where they would live. She would see them again eventually, so she didn't mind saying goodbye. They would be all right.

"Another good deed," the old woman said to herself as they ascended the glass stairs.

She drank the mug of broth and ate the bowl of ice cream that the girl had rejected. It was nice to have visitors sometimes, but she preferred to be alone so she could think. Her life had been so long, but it took so much time to understand anything.

More shadows would come, drawn by the blue light. The old woman suspected they thought it was a television, that they remembered watching reruns in the middle of the night. The old woman remembered being a girl, her mother turning on the television when she was sick and sad. The shadows were drawn to her house as to a place of comfort.

The girl had been wise. After eating her mother, she had washed herself, and she had avoided the traps of monsters, the chunks of their flesh and the baubles they left for the unsuspecting. What happened to the people upstairs? The old woman had no idea. It wasn't her business, and she had stopped asking for things.

Glass Mother

MY FRIEND ALISSA'S boyfriend disappeared, and her mother was dead, so she asked three of her friends to form a birthing committee. One friend's job was to coach her through the labor. Another friend's job was to cut the umbilical cord and watch the doctor for signs of malpractice. I was no good with blood or sweat or tears, so my job was to man her phone.

"Do you think I'll be a good mother?" Alissa kept asking in the weeks leading up to the delivery date.

"Yes, of course," I assured her again and again. I wasn't sure what it meant to be a good mother, or if anyone could be something so absolute, but I didn't trouble her with my philosophical qualms.

"When are you going to have a baby to be my baby's friend?" That was her other favorite question for me.

"I told you, I don't want to have a baby."

"The right man will come along."

"It doesn't matter if he does. It's just not my thing."

"You'll change your mind when you meet my baby," she said and said and said. But I didn't mind much. She was trying to convince herself she'd done the right thing.

She went into labor a week early, just after midnight, so I dragged myself out of bed and met her and her two other friends at the hospital. I should have been expecting the call, but I was in shock. My duty was relatively minor, yet I felt unprepared.

By the time I reached her hospital room and she handed me her phone, she was frantic with pain.

"Why don't you get an epidural?" I said. Her agony made me sweat.

"I want to, but I have to wait until I'm dilated enough. Oh God, I'm scared! I want my mother!"

She reached out for a glass figurine on her bedside table. It was a smiling, radiant woman made of frosted pink glass. Like a good witch, she had a wide-hemmed dress.

Alissa's friend who was her labor coach picked up the figurine and put it in Alissa's arms. She didn't hold it like a baby, but like a teddy bear. I began to regret not bringing a stuffed animal. I'd read that pain can make a person revert to a childlike state.

"What do you want me to tell everyone?" I said, deciding it would be polite to avoid commenting on whatever was happening and to focus on my assigned duties.

Her coach friend ignored me and told Alissa, "Your mother is here with you. Her spirit is hovering over you."

Alissa closed her eyes and smiled. A moment of silence passed, and I stood frozen in the doorway. Finally, she opened her eyes again and looked calmer, though she was crying a little.

"Why did my mom have to die? I loved her so much. I don't mind that Jeff left. He wouldn't have been that much help with the baby. But my mom would have been."

"That sucks," I said, walking closer to the bed. Her coach friend gave me a look of warning. "It's totally unfair."

"But we have to focus on the positive!" her friend said. "Your mother's spirit is here."

"And your dad will be here," I said, hoping to appease everyone with my positive thinking.

Alissa snorted. "He'll try to bring his wife."

She screamed out in pain again, as if the memory of her father's new wife had triggered another contraction. I waited while she endured this bout of pain, and her coach friend reassured her with the speed of an auctioneer that everything was all right, and that the pain would be over soon.

Once she recovered, she said, "Text my dad and tell him I'm in labor, but not to bring that witch." It was an awkward task that I didn't want to handle, but anything was better than being in the hospital room. Since she was between contractions, she asked me to take a picture of her smiling and holding the pink glass figurine.

"Post it on all my accounts and say that I'm in labor now, but I have this gift my mother gave me before she died. Her spirit is with me."

I agreed, and I went into the waiting room to conduct my business. Her third friend was taking a nap on one of the hard, germy-looking couches in the waiting room, so I didn't bother her. She was resting up for the big moment.

Once I had finished my texting and posting, I started getting phone calls. She hadn't told me whether I should answer her phone, but I did. I felt like an intern who was trying to get ahead by taking on extra responsibilities.

The first call came from her father, who told me that Alissa had strange notions sometimes, and that of course he was bringing his wife.

Several more calls came from more friends of Alissa's. One was from her ex-boyfriend's mother, who said she was very sorry for what had happened and hoped that Alissa would allow the baby to be in her life. I said I would pass along the message. I couldn't believe so many people were awake and responding to posts they'd seen in the middle of the night. Under the posts I'd made, so many people wished her well and shared vulnerable moments about their own grief and loss. I had to thank them all. The responses kept me occupied. I was her loyal secretary, waiting in the bunker while she went to war.

I got a call from someone labeled "Icemother" in Alissa's phone, and I had a guess about who it was before I answered.

"I'm on my way," Alissa's stepmother said, sounding steady and determined. Probably the husband hadn't even told her she wasn't welcome, because she didn't sound tentative at all.

"Hello?" I said, wondering how I was going to tell her she wasn't invited to the birth.

"Who are you?" she said.

"I'm Alissa's friend Ellen. I'm in charge of her phone while she's in labor."

"Splendid. I'll bring you some good coffee to help you stay awake. I'm also going to stop to buy flowers. My husband is going out to find a toy that will be the perfect first gift, but I thought it might be nice to bring flowers for the room."

"Sounds good," I said. I'd never discussed flowers with Alissa, but whenever her former boyfriend had sent her a flower arrangement, she'd posted pictures of it on all her social media accounts.

"I think I'll bring gray flowers," the Icemother said.

Was there such a thing as a gray flower? I felt so tired and confused, I wasn't sure. Either way, it didn't seem appropriate. I could see Alissa recoiling at the drab gift from the stepmother she hated.

"Maybe white flowers instead?" I said. I closed my eyes, and I could see a beautiful bouquet of white hydrangeas and roses and lilies and baby's breath. There was something antiseptic and fresh about a bouquet of white flowers. Alissa loved classic colors and styles, and I doubted she could resist a fresh bouquet of white.

"No, I think gray flowers will be just the thing," she said, disagreeing with me in the most pleasant tone. "Need anything else?"

"No," I said.

I knew Alissa would have wanted me to tell her she wasn't welcome, but I couldn't. I couldn't be so rude to a stranger who had never done me any harm. Alissa and I had talked endlessly about her hatred for her stepmother and my own hatred for my stepfather, but my stepfather hit me. Her stepmother was simply stiff and cold. She didn't hug, didn't compliment, didn't comfort. Not Alissa's idea of a stand-in for a mother. I would have preferred that kind of stepparent to the one I had, but you have to take your friend's side. Otherwise, who will take your side?

One thing I was certain of—it wasn't right that Alissa's mother had died so young. She needed her. I went back to Alissa's room with an update on all her well-wishers (leaving out the impending arrival of the Icemother and her gray flowers).

Her coach friend eyed me with suspicion when I entered the room, but Alissa waved me in. I had never paid much attention to her other friends before. I didn't have much in common with them. Of course, I didn't have much in common with Alissa either, but life had brought us together. We had become friends at our work at the accounting firm, where she was in customer service and I sat in the back with my math.

"Your name is Ann, right?" I asked the friend.

"Annie," she said, picking up her own phone and examining it. I'd seen her at Alissa's parties, but we'd never made more than small talk.

"I'm Ellen."

"I know."

"Good news, I'm going to get my epidural now!" Alissa said, interrupting our painful conversation. "Thanks so much for everything. You guys are my rocks. Without you, I couldn't do this."

The pink glass woman was standing on the nightstand again, presiding over everything.

"Annie, why don't you take a quick break? Ellen will keep me company for a minute."

Annie gave her a smile and avoided eye contact with me as she jogged out of the room. She looked like someone who jogged everywhere.

"Does she dislike me for some reason?" I asked Alissa.

"Oh no! She doesn't know you. She just thinks vibes are really important for stuff like this. She's kind of superstitious."

"Oh, right." I must have given off bad vibes.

"She says you've never given birth, so you don't understand the…the spiritual enormity of it."

"That's true." I hoped I never had to understand it.

"But the thing is, the most spiritually enormous thing has already happened to me. I've never missed my mother more than I do tonight. I know it's silly, but I'm scared. The doctors say everything is normal, but what if I die? What if something is wrong with the baby?" She reached one hand out to touch the glass figurine that was sitting on the bedside table again.

"I guess something's wrong with every baby," I said, but I quickly corrected myself. Those were exactly the vibes that had troubled Annie. "I mean, nothing's perfect. But so far, everything has gone according to plan. You're doing really well!"

"Did you talk to my dad?"

"He's on his way! He's just stopping to get a toy first for some reason."

"Oh. He always thinks spending money is the answer. And his wife isn't coming, right?"

"The Icemother?" I said, and we laughed like conspirators. "She wasn't in the car with him."

"That's good. I can't see her tonight. I feel like…my mother's blessing is still with me. But if *she* comes in, it'll go away. I can't explain it."

"That's okay. I understand." I didn't understand. "I mean, this glass doll…it came from your mother, you said?"

"She said I should always keep it near me, and that she'd always be there. I know you don't believe in that kind of stuff."

"I'm not sure what I believe," I said.

"I always sense her presence when I have it with me. I know it seems funny. It's just a cheap thing. It makes me seem like a little girl. But I really think she's there inside of it. Some part of her spirit is, anyway."

I looked at the doll. I wanted to pick it up and examine it for signs of a partial soul, but I was afraid I'd drop it. Annie returned to the room and said it was time for the epidural, so I got out as quickly as I could. I didn't want to see that needle. Before I left, Alissa asked me to update her accounts with the news that she was about to have the baby, and to wake up her friend Jan.

I returned to my post in the waiting room, and when I woke Jan, she got to her feet like the room was on fire.

My update was met with many hearts, many prayer hands, many happy faces. I didn't have nearly as many friends as Alissa. The idea of having to tell so many people what was happening to me made me feel queasy. It was fun to experience vicariously, though. It was like I could pretend to be my friend for the night. I added a lot of exclamation points to the posts, and I said things like, "I can't wait to meet my new best friend." It was the kind of thing I'd heard her say the whole time she'd been pregnant. I even said, "I know my mother's spirit is guiding me now."

Time passed quickly as I liked each friendly reply, and before I knew it, a regal-looking woman stood before me. She held a clear vase full of gray flowers, and she handed me a cup of coffee.

I was transfixed by the flowers. If she hadn't told me they were gray, I might not have called them that. The bouquet was made of light lavender-looking roses and darker lavender irises and some silvery bits of eucalyptus. Somehow by calling it gray, it helped me see in gray, especially when displayed against the Icemother's outfit. She wore a dark gray dress with matching pumps, and her gray hair was perfectly arranged.

"Aren't you impressed I was able to get these at the crack of dawn?"

I nodded.

"I know the most reliable and intelligent florist. I'll have to write her name down for you before this is all over."

"Oh, great! I never give flowers, but I suppose it could be a good idea." They always seemed impractical to me.

"You never know when they might be needed. But no doubt, you have your own gifts to bring."

I was impressed by the flowers, but I knew Alissa would not be. I couldn't help but be drawn to this woman, and I didn't want to disappoint her by telling her that her stepdaughter didn't want to see her.

"Please have a seat, they're just putting in the epidural now."

She sat beside me, the water sloshing around in the crystal vase she held. It must have been one of her own vases since it was nicer than anything I'd seen in a flower shop.

"Where is your husband?" I said.

"Still looking for that toy. He says it has to symbolize his hopes for the child. Something like an airplane or rocket ship. Something that soars high."

"Oh. That's good."

I was fiddling with Alissa's phone, turning it around and around as I thought of what to say. I was very nervous about telling this stately older woman that she wasn't allowed to go backstage. Who was I to interfere?

"You're like me, aren't you?" she said.

"I'd like to be," I said without thinking. It was a strange question for her to ask, and a strange way for me to answer. But I was beginning to think we were alike in some ways, and that maybe I could speak freely with her.

"We're all becoming something, slowly," she said.

"Sometimes I wish I could become something in particular." I knew I was being unclear. I didn't mean that I wanted a promotion at work or to get married or become a mother. I meant that sometimes I wanted to participate at the center of things instead of always on the fringes.

"You are," she said simply, as if she knew me as well as God or my mother. "We all have to answer the phone for other people or get them coffee sometimes. That isn't all we are."

I took a sip of the coffee she'd given me and nodded. Above all, I wanted to be honest.

"I have to tell you something," I said, my voice wavering. "Alissa misses her mother. It's nothing personal, but see, she sort of wants privacy right now."

The Icemother turned to face me and gave me a coy smile. "What do you mean? Speak out! I know her father's going to go back to see her when he gets here."

"But see, since you're her stepmother, she might feel weird about you going back there. She wants to feel like the spirit of her mother is there. I know that might sound silly."

"I understand. She hates me! I don't mind." I could tell she meant what she said.

"Oh, good!" I eased back in my seat and put down Alissa's phone.

"But I had to bring these flowers. And I had to come so I could give my blessing."

"Your blessing?"

Alissa had seemed to believe her stepmother's blessing would interfere with her mother's blessing. I wondered if that was true, if one had a cold spell and the other had a hot spell, so that they would cancel each other out. Blessings seemed to exist on another level with angels and fairies. Maybe it wasn't such a crazy idea.

"You're here to give your blessing, too. Don't you think Alissa could have handled her own phone? I've seen her use her phone when she had two broken arms. She wanted you here, though."

"So I could give my blessing?"

She nodded. "If I don't give my blessing, who knows what might happen? This child might prick her finger one day and sleep for a hundred years. What do you think will happen if you don't give your blessing?"

We sat in silence for a time, and I wondered what might happen to the child in years to come. I couldn't bear the thought of her being exposed to all the prickly garbage in the world.

My thoughts were interrupted when Alissa's father arrived with a box of donuts to share, and he showed off his gift of a toy eagle whose wings were the size of his hands. Once the child was eight or ten, she might begin to play with it. Until then, it would sit as a good omen on the child's dresser, the way Alissa's pink glass mother sat on hers.

Soon Annie emerged and said the baby had arrived. She addressed this information to Alissa's father, avoiding eye contact with the Icemother and me.

"You go first," I told him. "I'll go in a minute." I wanted to give him a chance to do whatever people did in those early moments when initiating a new person in their family. Then I would go in and see my friend.

Once he left us, the Icemother said, "There is a kind of magic at work in there. It sounds silly, but I've come to believe it's true. But you know, we have another kind of magic."

"What kind?"

She handed me her vase of gray flowers. When I went in to see Alissa, I put the gift on her windowsill and didn't tell her where it came from. It was better if she didn't know. Her mother's spirit cast her pink light over the hospital room, and the Icemother cast her gray light, though both women were absent from the room.

Glass Book

Documentary night at the bookstore, so Singe had to stock the shelves soundlessly as TVs on every floor played a Rick Steves' Travel Special called *Europe: The Fruits of Conquest*. She had been instructed to set up hundreds of folding chairs for the occasion, but only two or three chairs on each floor were occupied.

As she put the books in their proper places, she listened to the blather of rain on the windows behind the cheery sounds of the documentary. She was sleepy, but there was no time to sleep, so she descended the nine sets of stairs to the warehouse basement to gather more books to shelve.

The Sorter had strange ways. Singe didn't always agree with the Sorter's methods, but she thanked God that she didn't have to do the sorting. The Sorter had placed six books under the giant Electricity sign, but as she carried them to the Electricity section on the 12th floor, she noticed their titles. They were either self-help books like *Spirits Are a Hassle* or romantic-looking books like *Dimmy's Last Dance*. None of them were science books. Maybe the Sorter found spirits and dancing to be electric. It was none of her business, so she put the books on the shelves alphabetically according to their titles. She was glad she had never met her manager, the Sorter. Sometimes when she went down for more books, she'd find one she already shelved. That was how she knew she'd made a mistake.

Meanwhile, that night, the loudspeaker played a quiet fight between the cashier named Port and the cashier's manager, Tim. They argued over whether apples could be accepted in exchange for books, a mistake that Port had apparently made. "These apples are of the finest quality. Look!" Port kept saying. It seemed to be his only argument. In response, Tim recited Bible verses in harsh whispers. The customers were undeterred by the noise as they watched Rick Steves, but it addled Singe's brain and made it hard for her to alphabetize.

Strange events always accompanied documentary nights. During a showing of *Owls: The Sky Is Their Bathroom,* Singe had found a lover. Or the lover had found her. It was hard to understand, but they saw each other while Singe was stocking, and they found themselves kissing in a nook between the Shape section and the Greece section. That was a nice surprise, but it was soon over. The customer came back once after that but pretended not to notice Singe stocking a second time. Love came and went, which Singe thought someone needed to write a book about.

Later, Singe met her mother's ghost during a showing of *The Hundred Years' Spaghetti War*. She was kind of interested in the war, so she tried to watch the documentary as she slowly stocked books. While engrossed in the film, she felt a soft substance like temperature-neutral snow falling on her head.

"Mother?" she said. She knew somehow.

The flaky substance evaporated, and she heard her mother's voice say, "Sorry to bother you."

No one else seemed to hear. Many people had come to see that particular documentary, and none turned their heads when the ghost of Singe's mother spoke.

"You aren't bothering me!" Singe whispered to her mother. But that was that. Her mother had left her again.

The Owner was often present on documentary nights, and once during a showing of *The Speed of Speed*, Singe had passed him on the stairs. He'd worn yellow pants and a yellow shirt, and he was so even-featured and had such kind eyes, he could have hosted a documentary. He'd been followed by several managers who'd kept up a constant murmur of praise for him, and they'd looked angrily at Singe for daring to go down the stairs when they were going up the stairs, but the Owner had smiled at her. Smiled at her.

Singe knew to expect the unexpected that night. And yet, things had been rather uneventful. When she was done in Electricity, she found a stack of books that took her to the fourteenth floor to the Remorse section. This was quite a large section. Many books were somehow on that subject, even if it wasn't obvious to Singe based on the covers. The Sorter knew. Singe had no time to read books. The ones who read them worked on a different floor, one very high up that Singe had never seen but had only heard about from arguments over the loudspeaker.

The documentary went on, from Germany to France to Italy. The night grew darker, and the rain fell softer than before. Things were winding down.

"Maybe nothing will happen tonight," Singe said with a mixture of relief and disappointment. When something new happened to her, it was always painful, but it was also…something else. Like feeling the wind in your wings, like fighting, like sightseeing. Like speed.

She wished she could have some of Port's apple. On her next break (when would that be?) she would ask him to cut her a slice.

On her way down the stairs for another stack of books, she met someone in a gray robe that covered their body and face. Only their muscular arms were visible. They held a big black bag.

"Hello?" Singe said. She always greeted those she passed, unless it was the Owner, which would have been presumptuous.

They opened the bag and gestured for Singe to look inside. Apples. They had a pile of apples in the bag.

"You must be the customer Port was talking about," she said, smiling to herself. But she stopped, because she didn't want anyone to think the workers talked behind the customers' backs.

The customer said nothing, but reached beneath the pile of apples (Singe smelled the sweet skin, craved the crisp juice) and pulled out a glass book to place in her hands.

"What's that?" Singe said, even though she knew it was a glass book she was holding in her hands. That is, it was a glass object in the shape of a book. It smelled like apples.

No response. The customer closed the bag and ran down the stairs.

There were tiny windows in the stairwell, and a nearby streetlight barely shone through the small opening, and orange light made the glass book glow. It was heavy like a paperweight, but it was the size and shape of an ordinary hardback book.

The customer paid Port with an apple and in exchange received a book. What did it mean that the customer had given Singe a glass book in exchange for nothing at all? Was she in the customer's debt?

She wanted the book, though. She hid it under her coat in one of her big inner pockets and felt like she was shoplifting.

With a shudder, she remembered what had happened to the last shoplifter. Well, that would never happen to her. She could always say she was just on her way to stock the book.

In the warehouse basement, she saw a pile had been prepared for her under the giant Dust sign, and, to her surprise, a glass book was in the pile.

Her heart shook. She reached into her coat and discovered that the glass book was gone. Like it had never been there. The purpose and meaning of the glass book had been unclear to her, but still, it had been special. She knew that.

She picked up her pile of books, trying not to look surprised (the Sorter was watching her, that much was clear, and her unsteady legs somehow took her to the eleventh floor. To the Dust section.

The other books were easy to alphabetize and sort, so she did them first. What about the glass book, which had no visible title or author? The thought of keeping the book for herself was tempting, but she simply put it at the beginning of the section. The clear book would be first.

Slowly, she descended the stairs to the basement for more books. So what? The glass book had been hers for a moment, and then it hadn't. It was never hers, but she had gotten to know it a little, to watch it fill with orange light from the window and to feel its heft.

Her new stack of books was under the Crow sign, so she grabbed the books and made her way to the seventeenth floor. It was good to have work to occupy her mind.

As she alphabetized the Crow books (first *A Tempter's Tale*, then *Anecdote of Madness*), her documentary night surprise finally arrived in the form of an announcement over the intercom.

The fight between Port and Tim was interrupted by someone with a clear, commanding voice. He asked, "Which employee left a glass book in the stacks? I am in love with you and wish to meet you."

Singe gasped. She knew it was the Owner's voice because she'd heard it in her dreams.

The customers ignored the hubbub, focusing on the documentary, but all the employees left their stations and ran down the stairs. Singe hadn't moved quickly enough. She found herself at the back of the crowd. On the bottom floor, the owner sat in a humble folding chair holding the beautiful glass book. A line had formed, and the first employee (a stranger to her) took the book in her hands. A buzz, and then smoke issued from the contact between glass and flesh. The employee shivered and fell. The Owner caught the book before it could shatter.

"Call an ambulance!" he said. "This book must be magic. Please don't come for the book if it isn't yours, or you see what might happen."

The poor employee was taken away in an ambulance. Singe hoped she survived. The other employees murmured to each other, and then one-by-one, they got out of line. Singe wasn't sure what to do. Had the book been hers? It had at least been in her possession. She would explain to the Owner what had happened, and he would tell her what to do.

Shyly, she approached him. She looked down at her white coat and saw it was smudged with ashes. Was it newsprint? No, she never stocked newspapers. Willie did that. Oh, why hadn't she looked in the mirror to check herself? Maybe on the Documentary Night when she'd met her mother's ghost, her mother had smeared her with her ashes. It was so hard to keep track of what she looked like when she had so much stocking to do.

Before she could approach him, the Owner looked down at the floor.

"I hear a voice," the Owner said. He looked at Singe, the only employee left in line. "Do you hear?"

No, nothing. She heard nothing.

"I believe not," she said.

"It is the voice of the Sorter."

"Oh, where?" She listened with all her might. She had longed to hear her manager's voice, but she had given it up as a childish want. She had doubted at times whether the Sorter was real. And yet, she had always admired the *Owner*. The Sorter was so irrational, so annoying. She didn't want to think the Sorter's strange choices had been made by the Owner.

"There it is. She says that the book is hers."

"But…how? A customer gave it to me from their apples. I think it was a gift, see. Smells like apples," Singe said, her tongue lost its way as she spoke to the Owner, who was more beautiful the more she approached.

"She says you stole it from her."

"Stole?" Singe stepped back. "The last person accused of stealing was…well…"

"It happened while I was gone," the Owner said, his twilight violet eyes shining with tears. "I wouldn't have wanted that."

"All over the floor, and then," Singe continued, seeing it in her head. But she had run away before it was finished.

"Yes, the supreme night manager responsible for that is no longer here," the Owner said, bowing his tawny head. "My grandfather was very displeased."

"Your grandfather?"

"He's the Owner. He's made me a district manager. I know less than he knows."

"Oh." It was something she wished she didn't know. It was hard enough not knowing her manager, but she didn't even know the real Owner.

"I will not kill you. But stealing is a serious accusation. You are so innocent and lovely, I can hardly believe it," he said. His eyes blessed her with their understanding. She slipped into those eyes like someone in a book would slip into a river, cleaning themselves and splashing around.

She heard a chime at the front door. The customer with the gray cloak and strong arms had returned.

"You will tell them the truth!" Singe said.

The customer approached the Owner and whispered in his ear.

"So it was yours all along?" the Owner said, which made Singe want to cry. Of course, the book was the customer's, but the book had become hers. A gift. A transfer had been made.

Again, the customer whispered in the Owner's ear.

"So it was a gift?" the Owner said. "That is wonderful. Then the Sorter is lying."

The Owner called Tim and told him to get rid of the Sorter, to hire a new manager of that department. And to hire a new Singe.

"Come closer," he told Singe, and with bees in her heart, she did. "The book isn't really yours or the customer's. It's mine. I sold it, but I bought it back. I want to share it with you," he said. "I never should have sold it."

Singe nodded, not knowing what was happening, but wanting him and what belonged to him.

He held out the book, and she touched it. Electricity ran through her body, seemed to break it up and dry it out, and she felt the anguish of one who had been tricked. But then, it changed. She was no longer in the bookstore, but in the glass book. The glass ground there was marvelous, lit up by the orange light. The glass castle was spacious, and the Owner married her in one of its chapels. After their vows, she looked into the crowd and saw her mother's ghost. She saw the customer, too. Everyone clapped. So happy for her. Everyone thought that after all she'd been through, she deserved this world.

The story of the glass book was lovely. Was this reading, this living in the orange light among the glistening glass? It made her wonder what was in the other books.

She rested in the glass book. She laughed and ate and slept, and it was all so tiring. It was so tiring to look up and see the glittering glass stars at night. Where was the rain? The documentaries? She asked the Owner if she could have something to stock, like real books or glass books, or anything he pleased. He only laughed.

Was the Sorter dead? Had she loved the Sorter? These were the questions that plagued her as she lay on her warm glass bed. Maybe the new manager of her old department was better. Maybe they would tell her to put books in the right places. That was all she had ever wanted. If only she had known what she had wanted when she had been there and could have asked the Owner for that instead of the glass book.

But after more time passed, she grew less certain. Stocking books always, in the always night, it had been painful. It had been lonely. The Sorter had been evil. The customer had helped her. Her mother's spirit had been guiding her. She was lost, so she had to let the glass world take her. She had to let it creep over her like a frost, making her a glass girl. She had to feed the glass like death feeds mushrooms and life feeds apples. In the glass book, it always smelled like apples. Her mother's ghost came to see her sometimes, and they talked of nothing but the lovely smell.

Glass Clue

It was a glass clue, and that was all Joe knew about it. It was the size of his palm, a misshapen little ball. The glass seemed to have a slightly yellow tint, but it could have been his poor eyesight. He often saw colors wrong.

He discovered the clue underneath a coat he found lying on the forest floor. He tried moving leaves and stones that were near the coat, but he found no other clues.

When he searched the coat pockets, he found a pack of cigarettes and a bulletin for the First Baptist Church of Walson for a Sunday service that had taken place two weeks and two days prior.

Maybe it was Mr. Bright's coat, after all. Joe's mother would be happy to hear it, though it would also grieve her. That was how she always felt when her dire predictions came true: of two minds.

"You'll have to find Mr. Bright in the woods and give him a talking to so he won't do any more harm. I'd go out and do it myself if it weren't for my bad back." That was what she'd told him over the phone that morning.

"Who is he? What harm has he done?" Joe had said, which had annoyed his mother and caused her to make sounds that weren't words before she collected herself.

"I've told you and told you. I get a sense of things sometimes, but it isn't the kind of thing I could write a book about. If it weren't important, you wouldn't be hearing from me."

It was true, his mother didn't call every day. He went to her house once a week for Sunday dinner, and that was it. Most people in Walson saw their mothers every day.

So he told her he'd go into the woods near her house and look into the matter of Mr. Bright. She didn't ask for very much, really. Since he owned the grocery store, he'd take a guy off bagging duty a couple times a week and send him to her house with groceries. It wasn't clear to Joe why his mother didn't leave her house anymore. Her friends stayed at home, but they had more serious conditions, as far as he knew. She said her doctor thought she wasn't long for the world, but she wouldn't say why. Everything with her always had to be a mystery.

It was easy enough for him to send her food. It was another thing to embody her curiosity.

When he showed her the coat and glass blob, she assured him he'd done right. These belonged to Mr. Bright, and Joe had to track them to their source and be ready to fight. It was creepy when she talked that way since it reminded him of how spooky she could be when he was a kid and afraid of shadows. Now he was a man and didn't believe in spooky things. He was just humoring an old lady.

He waited until the next day to go to the evening service at the First Baptist Church of Walson. His mother was a Methodist, but now that he was grown, he always told her he was too busy for church. Neither of them had ever darkened the door of the first and only Southern Baptist church in town before.

Everyone knew him from the store, of course, and they were all very nice to him. He wasn't a fan of small talk, but he stood around the snack table until Pastor Clark sauntered over to him.

"Big Joe! What brings you to our humble church?" the pastor said. He had a gold chain around his neck, just visible through the collar of his white starched shirt, and his teeth were dazzling.

Joe wondered, *Mr. Bright? Pastor Bright?*

"Thank you for having me, Pastor. See, my mother's taken one of her notions."

"Uh oh!" the pastor's eyes went wide in comic fear.

"She sent me here to ask about something."

Joe showed the pastor the coat he'd found in the woods and asked if he'd seen anyone wearing a coat like that at a Sunday service two weeks prior.

Pastor Clark pretended to think, screwing up one eye and muttering to himself, but there would be no disguising a newcomer. Most people in town, and especially at the Baptist church, all knew each other.

"It's not a very unusual coat, Joe. Anyone might have been wearing it," the pastor said slowly. "But it was a packed house that night. We had a singing group down from Nashville. Probably all our members were there."

"Was there anyone in the crowd you didn't recognize? Who wasn't a member of the church?"

"I doubt it, but I can't recall," the pastor said. "Wish I could help you more. Want me to put it in the lost and found for you?"

The pastor gave him another glimpse of his snow-white teeth.

"Oh, no. I mean, eventually. But my mother would want me to keep checking."

Joe didn't ask the pastor about the glass blob. That was too strange to ask about, and the pastor might think there was something wrong with Joe and start coming to his house to see if he needed pastoring.

Later that night, Joe had a nightmare. He was decorating a Christmas tree, and he put a glass angel on top of the tree, and the angel glowed, and it was smiling. It was an ordinary tree topper, and Joe felt sort of bored in the dream. That is, until the angel's eyes opened, revealing a pair of empty eye sockets. Joe backed away from the Christmas tree, but the angel made the tree lean towards him.

He yelped in real life, and it woke him. He lay in the darkness for a while and told himself to calm down. He was getting jumpy like a little kid.

The angel had stared at him like he was hungry for him. What had he done to offend the angel? Maybe it was because he didn't go to church. He had nothing in particular against church, but his job at the grocery store wasn't exactly a Monday to Friday gig. He had to be in or nearby the store as much as possible to make sure everything about the place was clean and appealing.

He opened the drawer of his bedside table to check the glass blob to make sure it hadn't turned into an angel while he was sleeping. But no. It was still a fuzzy, undetermined shape. It reflected the little bit of moonlight pouring in from between the blinds, and it looked sort of pretty. It wasn't just a random piece of glass like you'd find in a knick-knack shop or shattered by a dumpster. It had that yellowish tint, like it was a gem or something. Maybe it was more than glass. Maybe it was more like a diamond.

No, not a diamond. A citrine. They were the yellow gems, the birthstones for November. He'd thought they would be cheap, but they were very expensive. It was easy to find cheap lookalikes, though. He didn't lie to his wife. She knew how much he'd taken from the bank account to buy it. It wasn't the most expensive thing in the world. It had looked so pretty, though, so old and sort of like amber. The glass clue was only a little yellow, whereas the stone he'd given his wife had looked like a glob of honey sweet enough to eat. The stone was still on her finger, whatever state her finger was in. Maybe it was mostly bone. It had been years and years.

It hurt him to think of her body in that state. He put the glass blob away and went back to sleep.

In the morning, the sky was full of thick clouds, and there was a hardness in the air. Autumn was threatening to turn to winter. He didn't have a good winter coat. He had a ratty old puffy coat he hadn't had time to replace. Might as well borrow Mr. Bright's coat.

It was a black peacoat, double-breasted. A nice-looking garment. He wore it and put the glass blob in the expansive pocket.

At the store, Gene the butcher ran up to Joe as he made his way to his office.

"That's my friend's coat!" Gene said.

"How do you know?" Joe said, feeling a little defensive about the coat, though he didn't know why. It wasn't really his, after all. It wasn't even his style, too preppy.

"He fixed it himself, see." Gene pointed to the hem of Joe's coat, which was sewed up with white thread. "This was the only thread he had. He kept complaining about it, but he never fixed it. He kept saying he wasn't long for this world anyway, so it didn't matter"

"Who was your friend?" At long last, the mystery would be solved, and then Joe could get back to work in earnest.

"My friend Paul. See, he…" Gene's voice got thick. "He died last week. Heart attack. His wife tried to wake him up, and he…well, he wouldn't. For months, he kept saying he was going to die. He got his affairs in order and even started getting religion. Wouldn't stop smoking or drinking, but God wouldn't ask a dying man to give up all his fun, right? I didn't even believe him when he said he was going to die. Thought he was being dramatic. Anyway, that's definitely his coat."

Joe felt cold in spite of the heavy coat and the store's well-functioning heater. He was wearing the coat of a dead man. He took it off right away.

He got the address from Gene and set out to talk to the man's wife. Maybe she'd appreciate having the coat (and the glass thing) returned to provide some kind of sentimental value. And his mother wasn't going to let the matter drop until he looked into it.

When Paul's wife answered the door, she seemed to have been waiting for him. She was wearing bright red lipstick and had a tray of coffee things arranged on the coffee table in the living room.

"Gene called me and told me about the coat," she said, seeming awfully happy and hospitable for a grieving widow. After Joe's wife died, he'd stayed in bed pretty much the whole time he wasn't at the grocery store.

"You ought to have it," Joe said, though he kept holding onto it.

She gestured for him to sit down, and she poured him a cup of coffee.

"I have a little Irish cream, too," she confessed with a giggle, gesturing to a small silver pitcher on the tray. Joe helped himself. The situation was making him a little nervous.

"I'm so sorry about your husband," he finally said after taking his first sip.

She looked down at her lap, and he could see a mixture of grief and guilt and excitement on her face. Was her husband Mr. Bright? Had he been cruel to her? Maybe she was happy to be free.

"He always told me he had special powers, but I never believed him. I wish I had listened."

"Powers?" He choked a little on his sweet coffee.

"I'll be honest with you. My husband was buried in that coat you're holding so tightly to. He always told everyone that nothing could keep him down for long. Well, he didn't stay down, did he?"

Joe hadn't noticed he was still clutching the coat with his free hand, keeping the thing on his lap. Once he heard it was the coat a man was buried in, he tossed it on the floor as fast as he could. Paul's wife scooped it up and held it to her chest like it had a heart and soul.

"Sorry. Sorry," Joe said. He put down his coffee cup and stood up. "I guess I'd better be going!"

He felt like he was going to throw up. It was too hot in Paul's old house.

"I'm so sorry," his wife said. "This must be a shock to you."

"I lost my wife, too. I know the mind plays strange tricks. You think of strange things."

Sometimes, Joe imagined his wife's citrine ring glowing inside the casket, lighting up her sleeping face. He hadn't wanted to think that all the life had been drained from that face. What was the point of having a face if it went away?

"It isn't all in my mind, though. You have his coat. How do you explain that?"

Joe kept his head down and kept talking. He needed to get out of that house. "I kept all my wife's things. I haven't thrown a thing away.

I'm not judging you, ma'am. I understand. I wish...I wish I'd kept the things I buried her with. To remember. You keep that coat. And there's something in the pocket, too."

Paul's wife reached into the right pocket and pulled out the glass blob. Each time Joe looked at it, it seemed to glow a little brighter.

"This must be his soul," his wife said, touching the glass to her cheek. It wasn't a cold blob of glass. Joe knew that. It always felt like someone had just been touching it and left a little of their blood's warmth on it. It was kept warm like an egg in a nest. For a little while, Joe had been the bird sitting on top of the nest. Now it would be the job of Paul's wife. It was her task now.

"Anyway, I hope you can find some comfort in all this. I should be getting back to work now."

Paul's wife had her ear to the glass blob. "Wait, Joe. Paul wants to thank you. He says he tried to get home to me, but he got tired along the way. If you hadn't come for him, he might have fallen asleep there forever in the woods."

"I'd better be getting back to work. No need to thank me."

"Just drop by the cemetery! His soul is here with me now, but since his body had to be buried there, that's where some part of him remains. He has something to show you. It'll just take a moment."

He hadn't felt so perplexed since the morning of his wife's death. Nothing about death made sense to him. On the way to the cemetery, he stopped by his mother's house to give her an update on the case. She didn't seem surprised by anything he told her.

"I knew that Mr. Bright was up to no good," she said.

"He came back for his wife, though."

There had been a crumpled feeling in Joe's heart since meeting Paul's wife, and he realized he was feeling jealous of her. Her husband had gone to all the trouble of making himself into a glass blob and donning his old coat to try to get back to her.

"People who mess with death are dangerously arrogant. Mark my words," his mother said.

"Jesus messed with death," Joe said.

"He did it to show us the right way to go about it. You have to go through the proper channels. Don't you think I've thought about all this? I'm on the threshold of death myself, and I have more insight than the average person, to say the least."

"So Mr. Bright is a bad guy for not going through the proper channels?"

"He's a bad guy, and that's why he didn't go through the proper channels. And you need to give him a talking to, or he might bring down a curse on the whole town. He might give the dead ideas."

His mother did look worse for wear, especially that morning. He'd knocked on her door before she'd gotten ready for the day, and with her face so gaunt and her eyes bulging, she reminded him of a wet cat. How would he feel when he got the news that she died? It would be a shock no matter what. Even when death walked right up to someone in broad daylight, like it was with his mother, it was always a shock to hear the news. Something about death just wasn't right. It didn't seem natural.

"I guess I've got to see this thing through," Joe said, and his mother agreed. So after using her phone to call the grocery store to tell them he'd be in a little later, he drove to the cemetery. He hated going there, though he made himself leave a new bunch of fake flowers at his wife's grave once a month. Real ones died too soon, and even the fake ones soon got sun-faded and wind-blown.

He wasn't sure where he'd find Paul, or Mr. Bright, so he parked at the perimeter and looked around. The day was still gray and chilly, and he didn't have a coat anymore, so he wrapped his arms around himself. There weren't any other mourners around that day. He felt quite alone.

"Paul?" he said aloud.

He thought he heard something, a sound like a coin falling to the floor. When he looked up, he saw a small yellow dot in the sky, like it was coming from a laser pointer. He tried to follow the source of the light, which led him over the tallest hill in the cemetery, the one with the three stone crosses that loomed above his head. Finally, he saw where the light was coming from.

On a bench near his own wife's grave, there sat two vague outlines of people. One was his wife, and he presumed the other was Paul. From the angle he was looking at, their hands seemed to touch. The yellow light was a reflection from the stone on his wife's hand.

He ran over to the pair, fierce blood pumping through his system. Yes, he would give that Mr. Bright a piece of his mind. How dare that man mess with something so sacred?

When he got closer, he saw their hands were not touching. His wife looked up and smiled at him. The coatless Paul gave him a wink.

Joe tried to punch Paul in the jaw, but of course his fist went right through that translucent face.

"Goddamn you, Mr. Bright," Joe said, or maybe shouted. He was crying by then. "Why did you have to go and do that? You're supposed to go through the proper channels."

Paul looked right at him and said (with a voice no higher than a whisper), "Who's to say I didn't?"

"You aren't supposed to violate things!" Joe shouted, wishing his mother were there. She'd know what to say. Joe still barely understood what had happened. He had a hard time looking at his wife's face.

Finally, he switched his attention and stared at her.

"I missed you," he said, sniveling like a child. He was embarrassed to look so weak in front of Mr. Bright.

"I missed you," she whispered. She smiled.

It didn't help. It didn't help one bit. Because then she was gone. It happened so fast. What was the point of it? Joe blinked, and his wife and Paul were both gone. Paul must have delivered his message, finished making his point.

On the bench where the ghost pair had sat, Joe looked down and found a sparkling object. It took his breath away. It was real, it was real! Solid as anything. It was his wife's citrine ring.

He held it in his hands. He whispered into it. He held it to its ear to see if it spoke back.

It was not as talkative as the glass blob left by Mr. Bright. But it was something. It was some piece of his wife. Some piece of her soul.

"But it isn't right!" he shouted at the empty spot where Mr. Bright had been.

He got no answer.

When he stared at the ring, he noticed it didn't glow as brightly as it had on her living finger. He tried to clean it with his shirt, but it was still dull. It didn't seem to catch the sunlight that burst every now and then from behind the clouds. When the light had shone from it before, it must have been lit by some invisible moon.

Joe put the ring in his pocket and went back to work. He prayed that his wife's soul would not be divided. He prayed he would die and find her whole in that other world.

The ring and the gemstone were so warm. He would ask his mother about it after work. Before she died, his mother would have to tell him the proper way to die. Otherwise, he was afraid that he might fall under the spell of Mr. Bright.

Glass Turtle

EVEN THOUGH THEIR house was only ten minutes from her college campus, Alice begged her mother to pay for a dorm room. She had to protect her mother, who was always so understanding even if she didn't understand.

"As long as you're over your bad boy phase, I guess I can let you be on your own," her mother said, winking.

The dorm room was bland and small, which was almost comforting. Her mother agreed to pay extra so she wouldn't have a roommate. She'd have a private little purgatory, a tiny gray womb where she could rest and begin again. She wasn't going to talk to anyone from high school. She was determined to only hang out with people in symphonic band. Unfortunately, it was in this zone of safety that she encountered Daniel.

Such a nice boy! He played the flute like she did, and he was first chair to her third chair, but he never mentioned it. On their third date, she figured she might as well fall in love with him when he ruined his good slacks to save a dog that had been hit by a car. He paid the bill at the emergency vet and took the dog to a local shelter where the scrappy little terrier could have a second chance.

"Why don't you adopt him?" Alice asked him. "He loves you."

"I live with my parents, and they wouldn't like it. We have a cat."

"Sometimes you can introduce a cat to a dog, and they make friends. I've seen it online."

He shook his head. "My parents aren't getting along right now. Can't rock the boat."

"Oh, I'm so sorry! My parents are divorced."

It was the kind of thing she wouldn't have told him without falling in love with him. She liked to keep her origins vague.

"Parents are tough," he said, shaking his head.

And that was all they said about it. He decided to change into his gym clothes and get cleaned up in her dorm bathroom, and then they went to the cafeteria that served pancakes all day. Afterwards, he asked if he could stay over. When she told him she wanted to wait, he seemed relieved. Later that week, she told him she loved him, and he said it back right away.

Her mother found out somehow. It was astonishing how her mother might know something that happened miles away but didn't know what was happening in her own house. But she had friends looking out for her on the outside. Inside the house, she seemed to go into a kind of trance. When she was with people, she fizzed like freshly-popped champagne, but when she was alone, she powered down. She could sit and stare at the ceiling or a spot on the wall and just disappear inside for a long time.

Alice and her mother had a standing appointment for breakfast every Sunday at the bagel place between campus and her house.

"I want to meet this new guy," her mother said while ripping her pink-and-purple striped bagel into shreds. "We used to be so close. You used to tell me everything. Now I have to find out everything from my friends. Is that why you won't come home? You're spending all your time with your boyfriend?"

Her high school boyfriend had once found a way inside her mother's house. Up a ladder, into her room. She had made the mistake of leaving the window open, and it would have been so embarrassing to call out for her mommy because she'd gotten herself into a scrape with a guy her mother had advised her not to date in the first place. Her mother had been right about Robert being a bad boy. It was worse than she thought, of course, and the closer Alice had gotten to him, the worse things turned out. It was too strange and sad to cope with. The things she'd found on his computer that time. The way he'd talked to her. All his bloody stories about the bullies who'd been after him his whole life. While she was remembering, her mother asked her what she was thinking about, so she shook the thoughts from her head.

She didn't want to introduce her mother to Daniel, but if she set that boundary, everyone would know something was wrong. Nothing needed to be wrong, so she agreed to bring Daniel to dinner at her mother's house that week. When she told him, he said he was happy to go.

It wasn't until they were pulling into the driveway of her old, hateful house that she began to wonder if she was putting her mom in danger. She didn't really know this guy.

"You do know him," she mouthed inaudibly to herself. "Animal lover. Kind. Flute." Of course she knew him. He was planning to be a lawyer.

Once they were inside, Alice was distracted by how much her mother had changed the house in the few months she'd been away. The living room was yellow instead of dark pink, and the old recliner was gone, and there was a hammock hanging from the ceiling.

"It's all different," Alice said, wanting to cry. It was impossible to say why these little changes, all for the better as far as she was concerned, would unnerve her.

"We have to give ourselves facelifts sometimes," her mother said, which triggered Alice to have one of her episodes.

Suddenly, it felt like she was unreal, in a dream or maybe in another reality from the one she'd started out in. She began to breathe too hard, but she kept Daniel and her mother from noticing by getting out an old photo album, which kept the two of them busy while Alice quietly talked herself out of her madness.

"Facelifts are when plastic surgeons smooth out your wrinkles," she reminded herself, moving her lips without vocalizing. "That's all.

That's all it is. Mom was talking about the house. Nothing to do with me. Nothing to do with me."

The oven dinged, which meant it was time for her to act very, very normal. Her mother led the way to the dining room, where she'd set the table with the pale blue napkins and tablecloth she remembered. It was so old. Why not get new ones, especially if she was going to paint over everything else?

Something bright and new caught her eye. She walked to the bay window her mother was so proud of and touched a little orange fabric bag hanging from a string of yellow ribbon that her mother had taped to the window frame. When she sniffed it, she smelled something earthy.

Her mother left the room for a minute and returned wearing her cow-print oven mitts and carrying a covered casserole dish. The salad was already on the table. Alice had forgotten to offer to help, which wasn't so unusual. Her mother caught her sniffing at the little bag.

"That's my new herb sachet! I got it from a hippie family I met in the town square. A family with two kids, and they're living out of a van! Can you believe it? I wonder where they go to the bathroom. Well anyway, it's a sachet for peace. It's got chamomile in it."

"You aren't supposed to make tea with it?" Daniel said, putting his arm around Alice to join in the sachet-viewing activity.

"Oh, no. It gives off good properties in the air, which keeps away bad things. Bad spirits, or maybe just bad feelings. Time to eat!" She uncovered the dish, revealing the messy chicken casserole she liked to make for guests. Even the smell of it made Alice nervous. Her father had always hated it.

"What do you two do for fun?" her mother asked them once their plates were full. Daniel politely paused to let Alice answer, but she couldn't conjure up any words, so he told some stories about the symphonic band.

Alice smiled and tried to look attentive, but she began to feel woozy, so she excused herself to go to the bathroom. She held tightly to the banister as she climbed the stairs to the second floor (where the hallway had been painted a creamed sunshine shade), and she felt herself drawn against her will to her old bedroom. She flicked the lights on and looked around, hoping her mother had changed everything. But no. It was the same as it had been the day she left it. Her mother never even rifled through her things.

Why didn't Alice's room deserve a facelift? Her mother had paid for the nose job Alice had asked for. There was nothing wrong with her old nose, except it was like her father's.

If it were Alice's house, she would have moved. She sure as hell would have thrown away those old blue napkins and that tablecloth. Alice knew where to look for the faint bloodstains, but no one else would have been able to see them. Her mother had gotten them out so well. Maybe she kept them to remind herself that she could get anything out.

Alice wished she had a sachet of herbs like her mother had. Maybe she just needed some inanimate object to give her confidence, which was the key to a comfortable life. Wasn't there some scrap of something, something to remember her own strength? She looked at her shelf of figurines, and one thing sparkled silently. A tiny glass turtle with an aquamarine tint. Her mother had bought it for her during their trip to the beach while their father was at home packing up his things. Just before her mother tried to get the restraining order, which didn't work for some reason. Alice was never sure why. She was in middle school at the time, and the whole thing made her want to become a lawyer when she grew up, but she realized she wouldn't have been good at it. She and her mom couldn't get their own legal matters sorted.

She put the turtle in the front pocket of her jeans (such a small turtle, it barely made a lump), and she went downstairs to take her place at the table.

"I didn't hear the toilet flush," her mother said, which made Alice gasp. Her mother gave her an impish grin. She'd gotten a pixie haircut about five years prior, and it had made her puckish.

"I had to wash my face," she said, and she thought of how she could change the subject. "Did you guys talk about school?"

Her mother's grin froze. "Of course! We've been talking about nothing but. Where has your head been, kid?" She was using her Humphrey Bogart voice, her swagger.

"I told her about our last concert where that trombonist passed out," Daniel said, giving Alice a comforting smile. He never teased her.

"Oh yeah! That was scary."

"And you gave him first aid!" Daniel said, encouraging her to brag.

"Alice always was a quick thinker," her mother said. "But you'll have to get Daniel to give you some tips on the flute. Maybe you can share that first chair!"

"Ha, sure," Alice said. She didn't want to be first chair, but it made Daniel uncomfortable when someone pointed out that he was ahead of her. He chewed his chicken casserole more quickly and spooned a little more onto his plate to distract himself.

They sat in silence for a minute.

"I'm sorry Alice doesn't have a father to introduce you to," her mother said. Alice almost dropped her fork. Her mother hadn't said anything like that since the separation. Since all of that.

"Oh," Daniel said. "Don't be! You're all she needs!"

Her mom gave him a strange look. "Every girl needs her father."

"God, Mom. That's so lame and not even true. Could we not, please?"

"Part of a healthy relationship is talking over the hard stuff."

Alice wanted to ask how she would know what a healthy relationship was like, but she kept her mouth shut.

"That's true," Daniel said. He was blushing, but he sounded confident. "Alice and I know that life isn't a bed of roses. You have to get real and talk things out."

Her mother looked appropriately pleased. "That's so true. Alice doesn't talk these things out with me. I worried she wouldn't know how."

His blush faded. He was really selling her mother on the idea that Alice was an open book. Alice hadn't said much about herself, though, except that her parents were divorced and her father wasn't in the picture. No specifics.

"She's told me about your struggles," he said. "I can't imagine living with a man like that. She is lucky she has you." He looked at her mother, and they shared some kind of sentimental smile. Unfortunately, he didn't stop there even though he'd already made his case.

"Alice is so poetic about her grief," he said, which would have made Alice laugh if he hadn't seemed so convinced. He thought he was telling the truth, no doubt. "One fascinating thing she said about her father is that he's a good person, but he was so good in the first place that he split himself into two parts."

She felt like she was dreaming. She had thought that very thing, but she'd never told Daniel.

"So interesting!" Her mother leaned forward.

He continued. "She said he was so gentle and kind, quiet as a mouse when she was young."

Her mother's eyes filled with tears. "I didn't think you remembered that," she said.

Alice wasn't sure what she remembered accurately about her father, but she was sure she hadn't mentioned any memories to Daniel. They'd fallen asleep while studying once, though. Had she talked in her sleep?

"One man was kind, and the other was cruel." Daniel's voice began to sound strange, like he had a cold, and his eyes lit up like they did when he was playing the flute.

"He became violent. Out of nowhere," her mother whispered. She used her napkin to wipe her eyes. "Where did the good man go?"

"I wonder," Daniel said. Alice didn't like the way he was looking at her, as if they were sharing a joke. There was nothing she found funny about him guessing her deepest fears and sharing them.

"What do you think, Alice?" her mother said, saying her name with the tenderness one usually reserves for a baby or pet.

"I think…" her voice broke. "I think he must be hiding somewhere."

"Where?" her mother said, sounding a bit frightened, like he might be hiding behind a curtain somewhere in the house.

"Not here," she assured her. "Somewhere else."

"He's moved on," Daniel assured them both.

Yes, he had moved on to someone else. Thank God, he seemed to have forgotten them, though Alice felt bad for his other family.

Daniel's phone rang, breaking the spell. He turned it off and apologized, but thankfully, it reminded everyone to move. They all got up from the table like they were rising out of bed. Daniel offered to help clean, but her mother told him that they'd done their part in keeping an old lady company. Alice told her she wasn't old, and her mother hugged her. She hugged Daniel, too. Alice couldn't remember the last time she'd felt so comfortable with her mother. As she and Daniel were walking out the door, her mother held her back for a second and whispered, "He's a keeper."

She smiled as if she knew what her mother meant. Really, she had never been so confused.

In the car, Daniel was silent at first, until Alice finally asked him how he'd guessed the thoughts she'd had about her father.

"You told me," he said.

"I'm sure I didn't. I don't like to talk about these kinds of things."

"It was after that concert at Loggins U. On the bus back. You were so sleepy," he said.

Alice knew that wasn't true. She had been sleepy, but she'd mostly listened to her headphones, and she hadn't talked to him about anything but the concert. Unless she was forgetting big chunks of time. Unless she was losing her mind.

They were back at her dorm in no time, and Alice said she had to study for a chemistry test in a couple of days, which was the truth. He kissed her goodbye and drove off. Like everything was normal.

Her stomach knotted as she climbed the stairs to her room. Something was wrong. One of them had made a mistake.

She wanted to study to distract herself from her foreboding feelings, but she was so exhausted, she went right to bed. Later, she swore she had locked the door before turning off the lights. The window was locked, too, and this time, Alice was on the third floor.

But in the middle of the night, she was disturbed from her sleep by the sound of the bed creaking. Someone else was there beside her.

Her first thought was that it was her ex, returning for another nightmare. That he'd pried the lock open. He was the only guy she knew with a knack for that kind of violation.

But she was wrong. She heard another voice.

"Thanks for letting me in, Alice," Daniel whispered in her ear.

"I didn't," she said. She didn't whisper. She didn't scream. She knew no one outside the room could hear her.

"Of course you did."

She didn't like to explain what happened after that, but she knew it meant she was alone in the world, frozen in an icicle. Everyone could see her.

He didn't say much afterwards, but he left right away. As soon as he slipped out the door, she locked it again and slid her desk across as an extra barrier. Maybe it wouldn't block him, but she could at least hear him enter.

She couldn't sleep after that, so she took a shower and washed her hair. She double-checked the locks and promised herself she'd make an appointment with a counselor on campus, but she wouldn't tell them the worst stuff. Otherwise, they might think something was really wrong with her.

At some point early in the morning, she fell asleep, and she didn't wake up again until around ten, after her first class. She soon learned that all her classes had been cancelled.

When she looked at her phone, she saw texts from her friends in band, alerts from the campus, and a string of frantic calls from her mother.

Daniel had died the night before in the woods near campus. When he didn't come home, his parents had called all his friends (they must not have known about Alice), and then the police. His body had been discovered and identified quickly. Everyone in the band was worried about Alice, so worried they told her they were sending up thousands of prayers.

She told everyone that she couldn't believe Daniel was gone. They took this for denial, the numbness of sudden grief. Was it a ghost who'd invaded her room, or had Daniel met his end after leaving her room? His father told the local news that if his mother had allowed Daniel to enlist, he would have been a war hero. Daniel had told Alice he wanted to tour with the symphony, but his father didn't seem to know about that.

Maybe everything said about Daniel was true. Certainly, her luck was off. She remembered the glass turtle she'd left in her discarded jeans and fished the little fellow out of her pocket. If only she'd left him on her nightstand. Maybe he would have guarded her, and none of it would have happened.

Her mother came to pick her up. Alice let her. On the ride home, she asked if she could sleep on the couch for a few days.

"But you have your room all ready for you," her mother said.

She shook her head and cried a little, so her mother didn't press it.

"Let me buy you something," she said. Alice tried to refuse, thinking it would be ice cream or another sweet distraction for a child, and she wasn't in the mood.

But she took her to the town square, to a van painted with swirls of red and blue. She pulled Alice out of the car and introduced her to the hippie dad. He was so kind, so helpful. Alice's mom told him what she knew, that Daniel had been found dead in the creek below a cliff, how some thought he'd been pushed while others thought he'd jumped. Alice didn't tell her part of the story, but she thought the man knew.

While the hippie father made the herb sachet, Alice and her mother waited in the sunshine and watched the man's daughters run around in the little veterans' park at the center of town. When he emerged from the van, the father handed Alice an orange pillow of chamomile, her own little sachet of peace.

"Hang it up or keep it with you if you're uneasy. Chamomile is one of our favorites to make. It means earth apple."

She was polite as he gave her his instructions, though she didn't care what the name meant. She thanked him, and her mother paid.

Alice was determined to return later for more sachets, more good feelings. She'd buy a lot of little objects that were sacred to her, a whole shelf of little glass animals. She promised herself that for the rest of her life, she'd do her part to keep evil away.

Later, when the police asked when she'd seen Daniel last, she said it was in his car after dinner with her mother. That was true. What happened after that was in the dark.

Glass Art

It is inevitable to have strong feelings about the artist Mirth Ivory. Whether you admire or despise him, you must admit he's changed everything. He was the first to show us patterns in the glass and to enclose his thoughts in glass. He rarely sits for interviews, but he owed me a favor, and I took advantage. I took advantage of him. If I'd known he would disappear after the interview, I would have never been so selfish. Or would I? I'm not a good person, though Mirth always said I was like orange glass. I thought it was a compliment. Now I'm not sure.

I suppose if my regrets were deep enough, I wouldn't print this interview.

Stan Tinch: Let's start with the most banal question a journalist can ask an artist. Were you an artistic child?

Mirth Ivory: You're an artist, too. Journalism is an art, and you were one of my favorite students. You used to paint your glass green like the excess of summer life. Remember?

ST: You're being interviewed, not me.

MI: Okay. As a kid, I made art out of balloons and razors and glue. That was all we had at the time.

ST: Your mother had a helium problem.

MI: Define problem. (He gave me a friendly smile to reassure me, and his aging skin creased like a chiffon gown.) But you're not being interviewed. To answer your question, I got interested in glass when I saw glass art that was painted by Tom Ransom and Bloomy Gland. My mother took me to see them at the circus, and she bought me my first four blobs of glass. One was painted green, one yellow, one orange, and one blue.

ST: Your mother had ambitions for you?

MI: No. She thought of me as a work of art.

ST: Art made by her?

MI: No. (He smiled again, but this time with his teeth.) By the end, she thought everyone was a work of art.

ST: That's something people often say. I wonder if they mean it. It's usually the biggest snobs who talk that way.

MI: Hard to say. At any rate, I loved those glass blobs, but an odd thing happened. I touched them so many times, my fingers wore the paint away.

ST: Some people might have repainted the glass blobs then or thrown them away.

MI: I kept them just as they were. That was when I noticed there was something inside them.

ST: Little eyes inside them?

MI: That's right. Little eyes all inside the glass. I thought there were little fairies inside the glass, and when I showed it to my mother, she was alarmed.

ST: Everyone was alarmed. It meant the glass was alive.

MI: Everything is alive.

ST: So you say. And once you spotted the little eyes and showed them to everyone, something strange happened.

MI: Yes. Once I spotted the eyes in the glass and showed it to others, the glass started to make its own color. The more people I showed each blob to, the brighter and more vivid the color would be.

ST: The first color you ever saw?

MI: Was orange. So beautiful. I always said I saw orange in your eyes. I see more tiny eyes in there, too. More than I've seen anywhere else.

ST: Are you attempting to flatter your interviewer?

MI: No.

ST: Some say you discovered the existence of souls.

MI: Yes.

ST: Do you believe that's what happened? That you discovered souls?

MI: No. I just saw them for the first time. Plenty of people knew about them.

ST: But not glass souls. And they didn't know one blob of glass contained hundreds of souls, and that noticing them could make them glow different colors?

MI: They didn't know that.

ST: Why did you notice? What makes you so special?

MI: I guess I noticed because I loved those glass blobs. I kept looking at them and touching them and looking at them some more.

ST: Can you properly be called an artist since you notice things instead of making things?

MI: I don't know.

ST: (I paused, trying to come up with a question that would really upset him.) Why do you think some of your students turned against you?

MI: You told me why you turned against me. You said I'd made you believe in a world that you couldn't get inside. It was driving you mad. You saw all the little eyes, what I call souls, but you couldn't get them to come out. And you couldn't go inside and get at them. It was beautiful at first for you, which was why you became my student, but eventually, it drove you mad. Some of us can stand on the outside, and some of us can't.

ST: I don't deny that I went mad. Now I'm sane again. I have a new career.

MI: That's wonderful. I want you to be happy.

ST: And yet some people couldn't ever see the colors or the tiny eyes. They couldn't see anything but simple glass.

MI: True.

ST: And it caused some controversy.

MI: It did.

ST: Do you feel guilty about all the arguments you caused? The violence?

MI: I wish it hadn't happened that way.

ST: Do you wish you had never seen the eyes and the colors?

MI: I can't say.

ST: You agreed to this interview! After all you did! All you did to me.

MI: I can only answer questions I know the answers to.

ST: I wish you had never found that other world. We would have all been better off.

MI: That's okay, Stan.

ST: (I began to cry. Mirth was silent, but he gave me a sympathetic look.)

MI: It's okay, Stan.

ST: But you don't care that you almost ruined my life?

MI: I care.

ST: But you aren't sure if you'd change anything?

MI: I'm glad that I found what I found inside the glass. Maybe I shouldn't have told anyone about it.

ST: I saw every color except one. There was one color you could see that I couldn't see.

MI: That's right. You couldn't see blue.

ST: I'd look into the glass you said was blue, and I'd see nothing. And you said that was the most important color.

MI: That's right.

ST: Why is blue the most important color?

MI: It means the glass is unnatural.

ST: Why? How do you know?

MI: My belief is that some colors of glass are natural. Orange glass. Yellow glass. Green glass. Pink glass. Even gray glass. But blue is unnatural.

ST: It's the color of the sky.

MI: Exactly.

ST: Where do all these colors come from?

MI: If I'd known that, I would have told you.

That was the last thing he said. The rest of the recording is just me shouting at him. I was so angry at him. I still am. Of all things, he died that night clutching a piece of glass that his students claimed was blue. At the funeral, they handed it to me and said he wanted me to have it.

What a monster he was to mock me after his death. I looked at the glass, and I saw glass. I keep looking for eyes and looking for colors, but I can't see anything. I can't even see the reflection of my own eyes.

Glass Coffins

I WAS DEPRESSED, so I went to the Gloweria, the VR mall for kids in the death scene. Mack dumped me, so I had to try something new. He told me he was tired of having a girlfriend, and he wouldn't explain it beyond that. It was more than a breakup—Mack made me who I was, and without him, I didn't see myself as a real person anymore. I was more like a ghost. After several weeks of hardcore mourning, I started reading about other subcultures and local experiences online. The Gloweria gave me some kind of hope.

Before our breakup, Mack and I always went to the Village Harmony Mall, the one closest to my house. That was where I'd spent every weekend of the previous four years with Mack. Every bit of it reminded me of him, with the soda kegs and late 20th century sports reels and kids in polo shirts and VR offerings of golf tournaments and yacht adventures and backyard cookouts that turn into brawls. It had all seemed so funny when I was with Mack.

I got into golf grandpa culture back in middle school because Mack was into it. He said his great-grandfather had actually won some kind of golf tournament, and he liked to celebrate the subculture semi-ironically. I always acted impressed by his family achievements. His dad was the mayor, after all, and Mack was indisputably an important person from a successful family, unlike me and mine.

While I was vaguely interested in other subcultures I'd noticed at school, like urchin zombie and hall monitor chic, it was hard to switch over. There are online guides to joining any subculture, but if you do what they say, people can sense you're not being real. The people in those groups won't accept you unless you can somehow adopt the style naturally. I already knew golf grandpa culture, and that's where all my friends were. But really, they were Mack's friends. I was only eighteen, and I'd lost myself before I'd ever found myself. I was determined to find a new self at the Gloweria.

The exterior was ordinary, plain concrete with cursive signage, probably to fool parents who were dropping off their kids. I parked in the deck, looking nervously at how everyone was dressed and how I didn't match. They were all wearing hats pulled low over their eyes and huge shapeless raincoats. I'd worn my darkest polo shirt and my most frayed-looking khakis to try to fit in until I could buy the right clothes at the Gloweria. I hoped no one gawked at me in the meantime.

I tried to act confident as I opened the giant dark-tinted double-doors, but right away, it felt like I'd made some mistake. There was no open atrium like in my local mall, no cheerful voices. Everyone spoke in whispers if they spoke at all.

The narrow hallway and fluorescent lights made you feel like you were entering a bland gray office complex where your psychologist or gymnotherapist was located; the difference was, the floor was made of glass, and beneath the glass there were glass coffins that displayed the bodies of dead (or sleeping?) famous people. There was Napoleon. And Madonna. And all four Beatles side-by-side in an extra-wide coffin. And Petey Eck. There was also the president (who obviously wasn't dead, so it seemed kind of cruel).

They all looked so peaceful, but it made you think. If those famous people were destined to die, how could I expect anything better?

I tried not to look too hard at the corpses. I knew they were just VR, but the tech was much better than it was at my regular mall. I was beginning to miss the faint taste of the virtual beer-flavored soda and the feel of a virtual golf club in my hands. I was one of the best grandpa golfers in my old mall, actually. The problem was, you weren't supposed to be good. It was just supposed to be funny. Still, I couldn't help trying to win.

All that to say, I managed to keep it together at first. I acted like I saw dead bodies under my feet every day. I had a harder time acting casual when the hallway began to darken. At first, the lights merely flickered overhead, but as I continued down the hall, I had to pass through a dark stretch. I bumped into someone, and then someone else. The first person yelled at me to watch out, and I yelled at the second person. I was determined to fit in. One thing Mack always hated about me was my determination. He said I didn't know how to relax and have fun, but what he didn't understand is that it takes determination to truly relax and have fun.

Finally, the dark hallway opened up into an indoor garden where honeysuckle vines crept over the shrubbery. In a clearing, there were little tea tables all set with scones and tea, but no one was seated. I took a seat at one, but a waiter approached me to ask if I had reservations, so I quickly scooted away. I hoped no one noticed my faux pas. I wanted to stay there in the garden and smell the flowers and grassy green tea, but everyone was moving on, and I had to follow.

I must have been smiling too much in the garden, because a shapeless figure in a raincoat and rainhat pointed at me and laughed, and then his friends laughed.

"Grandpa," they muttered, cracking themselves up. They thought they could see right through me.

I followed them past the garden and into another darkened hallway. First, I'd get a sense of the layout of the Gloweria, and then maybe I'd understand what the point was. Every subculture had some philosophy. Golf grandpas wanted to have fun, and they didn't care about suffering or anything. At the Gloweria, the deaths were obsessed with illusion as well as mortality. First the glass corpses filled with fake bodies…then the beautiful but empty garden. If the garden was like heaven, and I had no reservation there, then what was left for me?

All I could do was proceed, and I soon got used to the darkness. I kept my pace steady, and I didn't bump into anyone, and no one bumped into me.

The light returned when we turned a corner, and we found ourselves walking directly onto a stage. There was a large audience there to welcome us, and they applauded us as we walked across the stage. I knew they were just a VR crowd, and I'm embarrassed to say it, but it actually made me feel good to be applauded. There was a man on the stage with a stack of certificates, and he smiled warmly at each of us. When he handed me my certificate, it said: "Congratulations! You Are Dead, Kellin Hickman. Proceed to Floor 5."

It made me shiver to see my name written out. I wanted to ask how they knew my name, but I didn't want to seem clueless. They must have had some kind of scanner that saw through my pockets and wallet to read my ID. Obviously I wasn't dead.

I was starting to wonder if I was cut out for the death scene, but where else was I going to go? The next closest mall was in the next town, and it was for sex leprechauns, and I knew I'd never fit in with that subculture. Maybe I could pretend to be interested in death, too. I needed somewhere to fit in, and I needed it fast. Besides, how could I go backwards? There was nothing to do but make my way to Floor 5.

As we waited in the hallway for the elevator, someone finally directed a whisper at me. "Hey, you got Floor 5? That's so cool!"

He was a tall guy in a very rumpled suit, and his hat was so low over his face, I couldn't see the color of his eyes. Instead, I glanced at his certificate. He was Rich Griffin, and he'd been assigned to Floor 3.

"Oh yeah? What's on Floor 5?" I whispered back, trying to sound unimpressed.

"I don't know! Every time I come, I get assigned to Floor 2 or Floor 3. You must have done something really bad and interesting."

"Done something bad?"

"You get assigned a floor based on your sins. Didn't you know?"

"Honestly, it's my first time."

"What a way to start! Listen, when we're done, come meet me at the food court. I'll buy you lunch to celebrate your first day."

Even if he just wanted to be friends, it was a victory. I hadn't been invited to anything since Mack had dumped me.

"I'd like that," I said. "Where do I pay for this Floor 5 thing, though? No one's taken my money yet."

He lifted up his hat, and I caught my breath for a second. His eyes were the color of the sun shining into a cup of black tea.

"Don't worry," he said. "This part's free. I think there's some kind of advertising that pays for it all."

What did I have to lose, then? Whatever happened on Floor 5, I had something like a date waiting for me. When my turn finally came on the rickety-looking elevator, I said, "Floor 5, please," to the elevator attendant, a man in a trench coat who was wearing a mask that must have come from a witch costume.

"Kellin?" the attendant said. As the elevator closed, he took off his mask, and I felt like my soul leapt out of my body. The attendant was Mack, in the last place I ever expected to find him. It physically hurt to see him again.

"What?" I had so many questions for him, but I couldn't get them out.

"So you've found me out?" he said, his jaw tight.

"I came here to get away from you!" I said, wishing I'd never come at all. I should have just stayed in my room.

He pushed the emergency button, and the elevator lurched to a stop. The screech of the gears made me wonder if we were going to plunge.

"That doesn't make sense," he said. "I was trying to start over. You fit in so well as a golfer, but I had these deeper concerns, you know? About death. About the meaning of life. That's what led me here."

"You never said any of that to me."

"I couldn't! I thought you were too shallow."

"Well, I think about death all the time, and that's why I'm here," I said, even though what had really led me there was the need for new friends.

"I don't know what scheme you're trying, but I'm not getting back together with you. Ever. I'm actually seeing someone new."

"Me too," I said before my body had time to react to his words, before he could see the desperate shock on my face, as if he'd grabbed my hair and yanked.

He gave me his cold smirk, his favorite weapon. "It doesn't surprise me to hear you've moved on so quickly. You never gave a shit about me. You must be dating someone important to get assigned to Floor 5. I've never taken anyone there before."

I started to freeze up as I realized how afraid I was of Floor 5. What Mack and Rich considered cool would probably be horrifying for me. So far, there was nothing about the Gloweria that had pleased me. I was done with Mack, though. Truly done. I had no intention of asking him for advice.

"Look, I'm ready to go!" I told him, and so he put his mask on, pressed the fifth-floor button again, and ignored me for the rest of our brief journey.

When the doors opened, I actually forgot about him. At first glance, Floor 5 was just a room full of carnage, a splatter of blood and body parts.

As I stepped carefully into the room, I heard the elevator doors close behind me with cold indifference. I'd never felt more alone. I was in a two-car garage, and I realized it looked familiar. My bicycle was stuck in the corner beside the faded kiddie pool where I'd spent so many summers. This was my parents' garage, and someone had been mutilated there. I tried to look away from the bloody mess and focus on the familiar details, but ultimately, I was too curious.

The VR was stunning. It made the rest of the Gloweria (which was ten times more realistic than my normal mall) look like last generation's technology. I couldn't breathe through my nose because of the rancid smell of emptied bowels.

Then I had the worst feeling. I looked down at the floor at a disembodied hand that had been hacked off with some rough instrument, and there was something uncanny about it. I looked down at my own hands for comparison. The severed hand had my slightly-bulging knuckles and the H-shaped vein I had on my left hand. I knelt down, and something possessed me to actually pick up the hand. It was mine, after all.

"Hey, what is this?" I shouted, glancing around for help. I hoped someone in the Gloweria was watching. The hand was cold and stiff, the bone visible. Was this what it was like for Mack, all those years of holding my hand?

I wondered if this was some dirty trick of Mack's. Maybe he'd wanted to teach me a lesson. About what? Okay, I get it! Death is inevitable! But did it have to be like this?

Behind the kiddie pool, I saw a flash of dark brown hair. As I got closer, I saw it was even done up the way mine was that day—in a librarian bun that I thought might help me fit in with the death kids.

I couldn't stop myself. I picked up the severed head, holding it at a distance to avoid the little trickle of blood streaming from the gnarled neck.

My bun was so neat. I hadn't known when I left the house what a good job I'd done. I felt proud for a moment, in spite of the whole scene. Maybe if your last act is to make your hair into a bun, you have the right to be pleased with the result.

The eyes of my other head were closed, but they slowly opened and sized me up like I was a new girl at the lunch table. She didn't seem to recognize me. Did I always look so judgmental?

"Hey," I said to myself.

She mouthed something back, but I couldn't hear her. Her voice box was cut off.

"Say it again, and I'll read your lips," I said. I was a good lip reader.

"You are a fucking bitch," she mouthed, and it hurt. It was like if your mother called you a fucking bitch, or your boyfriend, or your teacher. It wasn't supposed to happen.

"I am you," I said. "You don't even know me!"

"I know you," she mouthed, frowning like I was quizzing her.

"Maybe you deserved this," I told her.

"I know," she said.

As she spoke those words, she disappeared in a theatrical little puff of smoke. Where there had been blood on my hands, now there was purple glitter. The bloody garage changed into a quiet dance club. No more blood and severed parts. Just women dancing, and all the women dancing were me. The music was heartfelt. On a small stage, a passionate woman was singing in a language I didn't recognize. She was me, too. I didn't know I could sing.

One of me came up to me and said, "Let's dance." I looked around. They were all wearing the same old polo shirt and khakis I was wearing, and they didn't look bad, but they didn't look comfortable either. The khakis were too long, and they kept tripping on the frayed hems. They didn't seem to mind, though. They were all letting loose, dancing in various styles to the sad chanteuse me and her small backup band of me.

"No," I said, and I walked over to the bar and asked myself for a drink. The bartender me poured out a glass of ginger ale.

"You're too young for the hard stuff," the bartender me said.

"Can I ask you a question?" I said.

"You already did."

"Ha. But seriously?"

"Sure. I'll do the best I can to answer."

"I'm just wondering...who am I? I mean, who are we?"

"There are many possibilities," the bartender me said.

"But I don't like that. I want there to be one answer," I said.

"But you aren't one thing. Think about it, okay? I have to go now, but I'll see you again soon." She winked at me. Wasn't she me?

With that, I was rudely ejected from Floor 5. The ground sank under me, and I tried to hold onto the bar, but it was slippery, and I plunged through the floor and into darkness. It felt like I was falling asleep. When I could see again, I was in a light, spacious atrium of an ordinary mall. There were shops full of shapeless attire, tarot cards, and thick books. People weren't whispering anymore. They were laughing. Had I died and gone to heaven? Was heaven just a mall?

"Hey Kellin!"

I turned around and saw Rich Griffin waving at me, and I absolutely ran towards him. He was sitting at a table in the food court, and he'd saved my seat with his hat and gathered two trays of food for us. Mostly fries covered with various kinds of goop.

I almost hugged him, but I decided to play it cool, so I gave him a high five instead. It was like he couldn't help but smile when he looked at me.

"Kellin Hickman! Her first time, and she gets invited to Floor 5. How was it? What happened up there?"

I laughed nervously, trying to figure out how to describe it and explain what it meant.

"I saw myself, like, murdered. And then there were a bunch of versions of myself. I guess it's because I'm trying to figure out—"

A horrible sight stopped my rambling. I looked down at the fries he'd bought, and the yellow and orange and chili goops were slowly changing color. Red. They were all turning red right before my eyes.

Panicked, I leaned down and smelled the fries, hoping it was just ketchup. No, it was a metallic smell. Probably my very own blood.

When I looked up at Rich for an explanation, his face was frozen in expectation, his eyes wide as a magician's after a trick.

"Are you hungry?" he said, leaning in for a kiss.

I pushed him away. I didn't care if the blood was fake—I didn't want to see it. It wasn't funny! It wasn't funny to make me see myself in pieces or eat bloody fries or be mocked just for wanting to fit in. Rich fit in. Mack fit in. They belonged in the Gloweria like fireflies belonged in a child's glass jar.

"I don't want this anymore," I shouted, running away from Rich as if I were being chased. Everyone in the foot court turned and stared at me, but I didn't care. I was getting out of there.

"Hey, wait!" Rich called after me. "Don't be so uptight! It was just a joke!"

He was still shouting after me, something about how to have fun, as I dashed through the nearest set of double doors leading out to the parking lot. I almost ran into a girl who was younger than me having a fight with her mom about whether she was old enough to enter.

"Stay away!" I told them. I ran back to my car, fumbling with my keys as I tried to unlock the door. It really felt like someone was chasing me. I sped away, though, and drove in silence for the fifteen minutes it took to get back to my house.

I parked in front of the house and ran inside, anxious to see my parents. They'd been worried about me since Mack dumped me, and I knew I could count on them to know what to say.

"Mom? Dad?" I called out, though I didn't see them in the house.

My mom emerged from the garage wearing her gardening clothes, which looked like they were stained with blood. The sight made me dizzy as I wondered whose blood it was.

"Oh, it's another one of you. God, who keeps sending new ones? We don't want a VR daughter. We want our real daughter back. But she's gone! As if that weren't bad enough, someone's played some kind of sick joke on us and recreated the crime scene. The police haven't been any help at all! Mack's family is so important. They can get away with anything. Why did they hate her so much? Why do they keep torturing us?"

She burst into tears. Mack's dad was the mayor, but his parents had always liked me. I hadn't heard from them since Mack dumped me, but I'd assumed they blamed Mack and not me for our breakup. I didn't want to see the garage. I didn't want to know what had happened. To calm my own nerves, I reassured my mom.

"Come on, Mom. Someone must have used some kind of VR device in the garage to make it look all bloody. It's fake!"

"If it's VR, why is it staining my clothes? Why would anyone make something that real?"

I'd never seen my mom look so anguished. She looked like someone had taken away the thing that mattered most to her. It was how I'd felt since the breakup.

My dad emerged from the garage next with the knees of his jeans soaked red, and he gave me a tentative smile.

"It's not the same, I know," he said, addressing my mom instead of me. "But she looks so much like her. So much like Kellin."

He walked over and gave me a hug. My mom looked miserable, but she followed him, and they both wrapped me up in their embrace.

I was frozen in fear. Was I still in the Gloweria? Yes, I must have been. But where did the Gloweria end, and where did my life begin?

I wish I had never heard about the place. Once you step into the wrong mall, there's no remedy. You can't un-enter. But maybe I could find a way out if I kept searching. Maybe I could find the staircase that would lead me down, down, down, and I could find an exit. The Gloweria had taught me something. In my desperation to belong, I'd finally found myself. I belonged as well as anyone. Everyone around me was in agony, and I fit right in.

Glass Museum

THE GLASS MAN'S head glowed like the tip of a struck match. July sun made the room prismatic. The sculpture was hung with invisible wires so that Don was at eye-level with it.

He knew he was supposed to be staring at the glass man and practicing his art appreciation, but he couldn't stop looking at the trees outside. Live oaks. They waved their frilly leaves at him.

"This guy looks impressive, I guess," Don said. "But I don't know what this is supposed to mean."

His brother Owen bent his gray head over the etched glass placard on the floor and read, "This piece is meant to show you how to look through the walls of your ego to the world beyond."

"Then why not just leave the glass man out of it?" Don said. "I can look at trees in my backyard."

Owen gave his small Owen-smile, one of his many ways of avoiding conversation.

They had gotten into the Glass Museum for free because it was the Day of Distinguished Veterans. Their war ribbons were all the admission they needed that day. It had seemed to Don like an activity for rich people, not two scraggly old veterans, but Owen had asked him to go with him. It was so rare that Owen asked him for anything.

As Don moved around, he could see the glass man's face more clearly. The cool-looking etched eyes, the sculpted lips—it gave him an eerie feeling.

"It reminds me of someone. Who is it?" Don said.

He let silence settle in, giving Owen the time he needed. Owen had been quiet even as a child, which had meant he wasn't much of a playmate.

"Looks kind of like a dead man who's been in the water. Or who's made of water," Owen said.

"Oh," Don said. They'd been friends with another pair of brothers when they were kids, and one had drowned. He didn't like to think about that, so he put it out of his mind.

They moved on to the next room, which featured a glass river. It stood frozen in mid-flow, stretching from one end of the plain white room to the other. Don stared at it for some indefinable amount of time, lost in its undulations.

"It says this piece is meant to show you that time can be frozen. It flows like a river, but it can be arrested." Owen said. He was being unusually chatty. Perhaps he was excited by the thrill of the occasion, a day of parades and special treatment.

"Must bring back memories for you," Don said. "You were guarding the Scaggs Bridge during the war. Scaggs River must have frozen over once or twice that winter?" The river had been a coveted assignment. Don had been in the desert, and the experience had left him with a slew of pock-marks on his forehead where the doctors had to keep carving out little skin cancers. No matter how hard he tried to keep himself in the shade and save his energy, he had always felt parched and scorched.

Owen nodded. "I asked to be there."

"You asked?" Don laughed. "Why would the army let a new recruit give himself an assignment?"

"I don't know," Owen said, smiling his most humble smile.

Everything had always come easily to Owen. He'd made the best grades and gotten into the best schools. He had more military awards than anyone Don knew. Their mother had always been so proud of Owen, her oldest boy. Don had prided himself in his ability to accept hard truths. He was not his mother's favorite. He was the less successful brother. And yet, he'd always had the feeling that in his lower status, he'd escaped something dreadful. In some stories, the prince gets turned into a beast, while the pauper has no trouble but his labor.

Don waited to see if Owen would say anything more about his wartime service, about the battle of Scaggs Bridge where hundreds of soldiers were slaughtered on each side. Because of his performance in that battle, Owen had received a gold ribbon, but he'd never told the story of his heroism to Don.

Instead, Owen walked out of the room and entered the next exhibit. The glass river was more pleasant to look at than the glass man, and Don hoped the next exhibit would be something uplifting. Life was hard enough, so why spend your free time looking at something depressing?

"What is this?" Don cried out when he entered the next room. The other rooms had made him uncomfortable for some reason, but at least they'd been simple and peaceful.

This room was dangerous. There were no columns or clear sculptures. The floor was covered with broken glass. There was a narrow pathway that was clear of glass, but Don noticed it too late.

"There must have been some kind of accident!" Don said. He examined the bottom of his shoe and found it coated in the glittering fragments.

"I'd say so," Owen said. "The placard says it's supposed to remind you that everything can be shattered in an instant and that no one is safe from pain or danger."

"How am I supposed to get this off my shoes? If I track it into the house, Ann'll kill me."

He looked up at Owen, and Owen wasn't wearing his usual humble look. He was glaring at Don. This was something new. He'd never seen Owen look the slightest bit angry.

"You don't always look where you step, do you, Don?"

"What?" Don began to back away from Owen until he stopped and reminded himself that it was just his big brother. Patient old Owen. Maybe he was playing a rare trick on him, some kind of holiday fun.

"I've been wanting to talk to you about it for some time." Owen said, that look of menace remaining on his face.

"About what?"

Owen grabbed him by the hand and yanked him into the next exhibit, where Don's glassy shoes couldn't gain traction on the marble floor, and Don slipped and fell hard.

"That hurt, goddamn it! I might have...I might have broken a hip!" Don was so shocked, his voice was shaking. He thought he was all right, but what if the fall had really hurt him? So many of his friends had been laid low by falls. He couldn't believe his brother could be so cruel. In spite of all his accomplishments, Owen had always seemed so wishy-washy. He did whatever their mother wanted. He did whatever anyone in charge told him to do. He couldn't think for himself. All these accusations, these hateful thoughts, burst into the center of Don's attention. It was like a snake had spit venom in his eyes, and he was full of burning. He wanted to take his brother and push him into a pile of broken glass.

Instead, Don screamed at him. "Have you lost your mind?"

No answer. Owen kept staring at him like he was a wolf about to gobble him up. Don managed to scrape the glass off of his shoes with his fingertips and stand up again. Without consulting Owen, he proceeded on to the next exhibit, determined to be done with the place as soon as possible.

At first, he thought they were back in the room with the glass man, but after staring at it for a minute, he realized that it was a smaller version. A glass child.

This time, he marched over to the placard and read it himself. There was something to this place. It was trying to tell him something.

"This piece of artwork is an innocent child, and he asks you an innocent question. Why did you hurt me? That's what the child is asking you now."

Don wondered if he had it in him to win a fistfight with his brother. When they were young, they'd both been brawlers, but now he was afraid he might fall and not get up again.

He had always been a good little brother. He'd never put Owen down or tried to work against him, no matter how often people compared him unfavorably to his older brother. Yet he could sense Owen's hatred. It seemed that the Glass Museum was a monument to his brother's hatred.

Owen's face took on a strange glow from the afternoon sun that blazed through the glass windows. He almost looked like an angel.

"Don't you have something to say, Don?"

"Did you make these glass things?"

"I designed them. Someone else made them."

It felt like a shard of glass had pierced his heart. After all these years, his silent brother had something to say to him, and instead of writing him a letter like an ordinary person, he'd designed a glass museum for him. There was no one like Owen. No one could compete with him.

"Why would you make a place like this?" Don said.

"Don't you have something to confess?"

"Not at all."

"You aren't this obtuse, Don."

Don found himself crying a few tears of shame. He had always wanted to make his brother proud.

"I didn't mean to hurt you," Don said. "Sure, I made fun of you sometimes behind your back. Maybe I tried to get people to like you less."

Owen took a step closer. "You weren't jealous of me. You could see how hard things were for me. It was lonely being praised. You wouldn't have traded places with me for the world."

Don wiped away his tears. "I guess that's right. I guess so."

"It's much easier to be you," Owen said. "You don't even have a conscience."

"How do you mean? We were both soldiers. And you killed a hell of a lot more people than I did."

There had been many protests against the war, and while soldiers were treated well in one sense with parades once a year, most people looked down on them. People saw the soldiers as violent monsters. But the truth was, those people were as responsible for the war as the soldiers were. They just hadn't gotten their hands dirty.

"You shouldn't have had any trouble killing enemies since you once killed a friend."

"A friend?"

"I know what you did to Peter."

Peter was the younger of the two brothers they'd once been friends with. After Peter had drowned, his family had moved out of town.

"I didn't do anything to him! It was an accident."

"I saw you hold his head underwater," Owen said.

"It was just a game! They said he had a seizure under there or something. How could I have known?"

"You hated him because he was stronger than you and smarter than you. Everyone liked him. Even I liked him more than I liked you."

"It isn't true!" Don said. He hadn't hated Peter. He was so young at the time that he hadn't believed anyone could be stronger or smarter than he was.

"He drowned because of you."

"But it was an accident. I was just horsing around."

Owen was breathing hard. He kept moving closer, and Don kept expecting him to throw a punch. Well, let him! Don had a chance of beating another old man in a fight.

His brother took so long thinking about it, though, that Don had time to make the first move. He'd always been faster. He slapped Owen hard, and then he turned around and ran.

There was only one way. He ran back through the broken glass (managing not to slip this time), and back through the room with the glass river, and past the looming glass man.

He still had it! It had been so long since he'd felt like a little boy, full of energy and spunk. He ran past the lady at the entrance desk, and she ran after him shouting, "Sir! Sir!"

But she couldn't catch up. Neither could Owen.

Don ran around the building, hiding from his brother. He'd always been the best at Hide and Seek.

From where he hid, he could see the glass man through the glass wall. He looked so silly inside his glass cage.

He found little acorns lying all around, and he picked them up and threw them at the glass wall. Then he found stones to throw. Soon, the glass wall was littered with little pock marks, just like the marks on his forehead. He'd always called them war wounds.

After throwing a handful of acorns, he realized he was crying. What was there to cry about? He'd gotten even with his brother. If only he hadn't been such a fool all along. He'd been tricked into going to the museum.

Finally, Owen found him. He put his hand on Don's throwing shoulder.

"I'm sorry, Don. I just wanted you to repent," he said.

"It was an accident," Don said. "Why can't you accept that?"

"I was in charge of you that day. I was in charge. It was all my fault."

Owen began to cry, too, and he pulled Don in for an embrace. But Don pulled away.

"I do have something to confess, Owen. I hate you. I've always hated you."

He left Owen there, crying outside his glass torture chamber. All designed to make Don repent.

So what if he had wanted that other child to die when he'd held him underwater, under the skin of the river? It didn't count against him. He had been so young. Before the war, he hadn't understood how fragile men were.

Glass Angel

THE ANGEL'S FACE was frozen in bliss, and Martha despised it. It was one of those saccharine figurines you find at a Christian bookstore, but Martha's mom acted like it belonged in a museum.

"Pray that God guides you on your journey. This angel will be a reminder of supernatural protection during these dangerous times," her mother said before launching into a description of the evils lurking in every crevice of a secular college campus.

Martha's graduation present was a glass angel the length of her forearm and a lecture about the lord of darkness. She pretended to appreciate these gifts. Her plan was to launch a private rebellion.

Her mother had tried to convince her to go to the local Christian college, a private school that offered Martha a scholarship since her late father had taught there. It was what her godly younger sister Mary was planning to do. Instead, Martha was going to the state university and taking out a loan. Her mother claimed her daughter's choices gave her heart palpitations. The glass angel was some kind of solution.

When she got to the dorm, she told her new roommate that her name was Alice. She knew she couldn't be Martha anymore.

Her roommate was named Stephanie, and she had a cough syrup addiction that she joked about all the time. It was a real addiction, though. She slept at least fifteen hours a day. So what? That was how much Alice's mother slept, too. It wasn't like it was evil or anything, and if it was evil, that probably meant that everyone was evil.

When Stephanie was awake for a meal, she'd go with Alice to the cafeteria for the all-day breakfast. Both of them started wearing pajamas all day, which Alice quickly realized was the freshman trend. College was one big slumber party. Soon she and Stephanie started hanging out with Leslie, another girl in the dorm who was majoring in pre-med and studied all the time.

"My family is pretty religious," Alice admitted to them one day. She took the glass angel out from its hiding place in her empty suitcase. "My mom said this was supposed to protect me or something."

"My parents are super religious, too. It's so stupid," Stephanie said.

Leslie's parents weren't religious, but they wouldn't allow a gram of sugar in their house, and they went running all the time.

"What's the point of living longer if you never have any fun?" Leslie asked them, and so the next day, Alice bought her a comically large candy bar, and the three of them split it while Stephanie occasionally took tiny sips of cough syrup. She told them she was down to twelve tiny sips a day.

It was what Alice had always dreamed of. A new family. Freedom. Shared misery. She kept her Bible in her suitcase with her glass angel.

It would have gone on this way, a path that led to a somewhat normal life, if she hadn't started hearing the angel's voice at night.

The voice came to her during the night after she'd eaten an experimental number of chocolate-covered espresso beans to study for a tough chemistry exam. The names of elements swam in her head, and she tried to quiet her mind, but she couldn't sleep. She snuck over to Stephanie's side of the room and found the cough syrup under her bed. She took a long swig.

While she waited for sleep, she heard a little whisper coming from the closet. It wasn't a fantasy sound. It was as real as the tiny particles she knew the names of but couldn't see. It must have been made of molecules, that sound.

The voice said, "Martha. Martha. Martha." It kept going. She covered her ears, but she could still hear it.

Stephanie was out cold on cough syrup and wouldn't have woken up for a fire alarm, so Alice felt a sense of privacy as she opened the suitcase and, with trembling hands, pulled out the offending angel. Was she losing her mind or having a religious experience? Either way, it was the last thing she wanted.

The glass angel seemed to glow a little like it had a tiny LED bulb inside, like an angel on top of a Christmas tree. And its lips moved. The glass around the lips was fluid somehow.

"Martha." The speaker stopped whispering and spoke in a normal voice. The voice was a familiar one she hadn't heard since she was eleven.

"Dad?"

"Martha, why do you forsake me?"

She was terrified, but she was angry, too, angry at the angel-dad. "Forsake me." It was just the kind of overwrought Scripture-quoting that he and her mother had always used to make her feel like they were God and she was a lowly sinner.

"You're the one who died!" she said, the sound of her voice so harsh, it startled her.

"You betrayed your family and God. You've turned your back on us," the angel continued. It was impossible to look at that strange face as its lips accused her.

She closed her eyes, took a deep breath, and gave herself a pep talk. "This isn't really happening. You just had too much caffeine and cough syrup. You're hallucinating. It'll all be okay in the morning if you go back to sleep."

After wrapping the angel (still jabbering in Bible verses) in a dirty t-shirt and putting it back in her suitcase, she returned to bed and put her pillow over her head. Her heart thudded in an off-measure. Was this a palpitation? She couldn't believe it was happening. She could still hear a little noise, like the sound of the television downstairs when her mother watched TV preachers in the middle of the night.

"Sleep. Sleep. Sleep," she told herself. It was an order. If she was ever going to what she wanted to do, she'd have to make her own voice more urgent than a message from God.

She didn't hear the strange voice when she woke up the next morning, so she rushed to get ready for class as if nothing had happened. The exam was a tough one, but she knew at least half of the answers without having to think too hard about them. Her mind was absorbed with the patterns and symbols of chemistry, which was why it surprised her so much to hear the voice again as she was finishing the exam.

"Why?" the voice said. "Why?"

She forced herself to smile at her professor as she turned in her exam, and she ran back to her dorm room. Stephanie was still asleep, so she was able to grab the glass angel from her suitcase unnoticed. She put it in a plastic shopping bag, grabbed the hammer Stephanie used to hang up her framed movie posters, and went to the back parking lot of the library. It was Friday afternoon, and no one was around to hear.

Utter privacy was what she needed to swing the hammer at the bag. She felt like she was breaking someone's bones. The glass shattered, and she disposed of the bag in a nearby dumpster and walked home feeling like her heart was all sweet and teased up like cotton candy.

Back at the dorm, she took a couple of swigs of Stephanie's cough syrup. The sky was easing into dusk, and it was still early, but Alice slept the sleep of the satisfied dead.

It was light outside when she opened her eyes to find Stephanie hovering over her.

"What's wrong?" she said to Stephanie in a sticky-sounding voice.

"Uh, it's three in the afternoon. You slept all day. I was worried about you."

"Oh, sorry."

"I hardly had any cough syrup this morning."

"Oh yeah. I took a little. Sorry!"

Stephanie just stared at her. She had never been so cold before. It felt like a bad dream.

"Okay, because it looks like you took a lot."

"I'll buy you more!" Alice said, desperate to make her feel better. Her friend was acting the way her mother did when she found Alice watching a show about witchcraft or talking to a boy who wasn't from their church.

"That's not the point," Stephanie said. "You know I'm trying to quit. Why would you start drinking it, too? It's like you don't even care!"

She grabbed her cough syrup and stormed out of the room, leaving Alice alone to make sense of what had happened to her. The angel was gone. Her roommate hated her. It was Saturday afternoon, and she had no plans. She tried calling Leslie, but she didn't answer. Probably she was consoling Stephanie and the two were talking about what a bad friend Alice was.

She took a shower in the bathroom down the hall and tried to feel clean again. It was like she'd had a wild night out, except all she'd done was drink some medicine and break a silly figurine. While she was staring at herself in the mirror, trying to figure out what to do with the night ahead, her mother called. Usually, she ignored her calls or answered just to say she was busy, but this time she was glad to have someone to talk to.

"I'm worried about you," her mother said. "I've been having dreams."

Alice was worried about herself. Maybe there was something to her mother's dreams.

"I broke the glass angel," she confessed.

Her mother didn't speak.

"I'm sorry, but I hated it. I hated it. I'm so sorry." She began to cry.

Her mother made a sound that could have been a sob but didn't respond.

"It was like it was…alive," she continued, knowing how she sounded. She sounded like her mother. "It was like it was possessed."

"You have to learn to resist the devil's voice sooner or later," her mother said. "I didn't learn until it was too late. I wanted you to learn young."

"The devil? But the voice was more like Dad's."

"You didn't know your father. He wasn't in the light of God."

Her mother had never spoken ill of her father before. It made her feel dizzy, like she couldn't tell which side was up. What had her father done to get out of the light? Was he in heaven or hell?

"What are you hiding?" Alice said.

"I've always sensed that you were like your father," her mother said. "I had prayed you would be made of something else. I thought the angel would be a way to test you. God would have helped you bear it patiently if you had asked."

"Why bear something patiently when I could throw it away?"

"That's just the kind of question he used to ask," her mother said, and she hung up the phone before Alice could respond.

Her mother had never given her a moment's peace before, and it turned out that all she had to do to be left alone was to be somehow like her father. What awful secrets her parents must have kept. They had seeped into her hair and skin and all her belongings. She didn't want to know her parents' secrets, but their molecules lingered in the air.

"Dad?" she whispered to the empty dorm room. But no one answered. The glass angel was gone.

The sun was setting as she went outside to take a walk around campus. It was mostly empty, with everyone either at home or at the bars. She didn't see anyone she knew. She didn't want to go back to the scene of the crime, the library parking lot where she'd destroyed the angel, and yet that was where she found herself. She looked around to see if any little pieces of glass were left on the ground. She peered into the dumpster and found that the bag of broken angel was still lying where she'd left it, barely pushed to the side by several garbage bags.

Tentatively, she pulled it out and looked inside. She imagined the angel would be ground to a fine powder given how hard she'd whacked it, but long broken shards remained so she could see the details of the angel's flowing dress and wind-swept hair. The face was still intact.

"Who are you?" she asked the angel. This time she wanted it to answer, even if it meant she was losing her mind.

The angel's lips moved a little, but she couldn't quite hear. She plucked the face from the bag and brought it close to her ear.

"Don't be afraid. You've found favor with God," the broken angel said.

It was what an angel had said to Mary before giving her the hard news that she was a pregnant virgin.

Alice began to cry. She stomped the face under the heel of her sneaker, which did nothing to crush it. This was what her parents had wanted for themselves and their children, to live out an ancient story that wasn't theirs, as if you could buy a cosmic destiny mass-produced. What small fingers had formed the angel, in what faraway place? But a banished soul could sleep anywhere. It could crawl into a cheap glass shape and spend eternity there.

"I hate you," she said.

The angel smiled up at her from the concrete.

"Now you believe," the angel said.

Looking Glass

WHEN I WAS TAKEN prisoner, I found a mirror affixed to the wall of my bedroom. I did not appear in the mirror, and neither did my canopy bed, my tapestry, or the trunk I was allowed to bring with me.

There was a wasteland in the mirror. Broken cobblestones took the place of my red-and-gold carpet, and gray sky took the place of my dark green walls. A frightened-looking girl took the place of my adult body. When I tried to smile at the girl, she wouldn't return my friendly looks. Her eyes were mostly white, like the eyes of a startled horse.

I could tell she saw my image instead of her own. She wore a ragged little tunic and dirty boots, but she kept trying to gather my thick skirt into a pile to sleep on and to pull my black shawl tighter around her shoulders. She was disappointed time and again. I wanted to help her, but how? I tried stepping through the mirror, but of course, it didn't yield.

The man who held me captive visited me each afternoon to give me French lessons. Each lesson took hours at first, because I kept interrupting to ask questions about the reason for my captivity and about the girl in the mirror. Eventually I gave up asking because he never answered, and the servant wouldn't bring my daily meal until the lesson was over. When he felt I had made progress, my captor left me alone to eat my meal, and I'd take it in front of the mirror. The girl had no food, but she pretended to eat with me, and her pantomime seemed to comfort her in the moment, though she always cried after I'd finished the food. I wanted to share real food with her, but how? At home, my father always told me of poor children who would have liked the food I refused, but when I proposed we take our food to them, he acted as though I'd missed the point. There was an impenetrable river between us and the poor, just as there was between us and the rich.

"The girl in the mirror is hungry. Please, let us feed her," I told my captor one day in such good French, he gave me a rare smile.

"You have a heavy Bavarian accent," he said. "But you can make yourself understood now. You're almost ready."

"For what?" I thought he wanted to host a party for his French friends, or maybe introduce me to his French family.

He didn't explain, and he didn't scold. He was a quiet man, shy. He rarely even looked me in the eyes.

After my father left me at the stranger's mansion for unknown reasons (all my father would say was that he owed the man), the first question I asked myself was…do I find my captor attractive? I thought that if I could find a way to fall in love with him, it would make things tolerable. Maybe I was excited by the mystery of him. I had no idea who any of his kin were, or how he'd gotten his fortune, or what kept him in our forest. He didn't seem to enjoy his lifestyle.

Before I met my captor, I had believed he would be frightful-looking, but he was only ordinary, a thin man who wore suspenders and glasses. I got the sense that he wouldn't have the energy to chase me down if I ever got away, but a tall stone wall circled his mansion, and the gate to escape was always locked. I checked that much, at least. At times, I wondered if I owed it to my father and my friends in the village to try harder to escape. My father had brought me to the mansion on horseback, and it hadn't taken long. I knew it wouldn't be a far walk to my village.

How could I leave the little girl in the mirror, though? I had to help her, to show her someone cared for her. I would never find her without my captor's help. She would suffer until I found a way to reach her.

Soon after my captor decided my French was acceptable, he told me I was going on a trip. Naturally, he didn't tell me where, but he did tell me not to take my trunk. It was to stay behind. I tried to tell the girl in the mirror that I would be gone for some time, but that I would be back. I told her I would help her. I spoke the words aloud, praying that the wind would carry them. When I spoke the words in German, she looked at me as if I were a donkey braying or a cat meowing. But when I mouthed in French, her eyes lit up for a moment.

"Do you speak French?" I mouthed in French.

She cocked her head. I spoke all the French words of comfort I knew, and I thought she almost smiled.

The next morning, I was excited to be going somewhere. I expected my captor to go with me, but he said he couldn't leave. I waited to see if he would kiss me goodbye. He approached me, some uninterpretable light gleaming in his eyes, and he told me I had to hurry so I wouldn't miss my train.

Out I went, wearing a simple dress and my favorite coat. After a ride in my captor's luxurious car, I entered a train headed towards Paris. As I traveled west, I also felt like I was traveling backwards in time. It was strange, but the train gave me time to think. Everything that had happened to me felt like something so old. In this new world, how could I have a captor? That was something that had happened to women long ago. So as I rode, I imagined I was becoming someone from long ago. In the past, we could summon magic. If I went back in time, I might relearn what my ancestors knew.

I wished I could meet someone who would ask me what was wrong with me. If even a mouse leapt into the seat beside me and started talking to me, I would have welcomed the company. At home, I could have asked my father or anyone else for advice, but on the train, I sat alone. People came and went, and they barely glanced at me. No one was coming to help me.

When I arrived at my destination—a train station on the outskirts of Paris—I wandered onto the platform and looked around, wondering where I'd go if I ran away. Maybe I'd go back to my father, or maybe I'd try to make friends in town.

Someone who worked for my captor found me, though. He wore a familiar servant's suit, and he rushed up to me as if we already knew each other.

He spoke to me in French, and he handed me a ticket. "This is for your trip home. Do you need me to hold onto it for you?"

"I'm not a child!" I said, hoping I could convey my dignity in my new language. I stuffed the ticket into my small purse.

"Come, I have the car waiting."

He led me to a car just like the one that dropped me off at the train station. It seemed that my captor had a large network of servants. I wondered how someone who never left his house could be so powerful.

I summoned the courage to ask him where we were going.

"To the place you have been asking for," he said.

I was puzzled at first. I had only asked him if I could go home or to see the girl in the looking glass. I had never asked to go to Paris. He said we were only in the outskirts of the city, in a place that had fallen on hard times.

This part of the city was all broken, with crumbled cobblestones and empty shops, and that was when I knew my request had been granted. This sky was the same dead gray as the one I saw in the mirror every morning.

"Can we find a bakery?" I asked him.

He obliged, finding the only bakery in the small town. The store was filled with gray-faced women waiting for bread, and they grumbled when the driver cut to the front of the line, but there was nothing they could do. I was served, and I asked for a bagful of pastries. My driver paid.

My heart began to flutter as I thought of taking this gift to the little girl. Food would be like gold to her. Maybe my captor would sneak into my bedroom and stare into the mirror to watch the scene unfold.

Maybe he would look longingly at my things left behind and pine for me.

When the driver turned onto an empty street, it was a most familiar scene. There, buildings had no doors. They had all turned their backs to us. This was the street I had stared at in the mirror since the beginning of my captivity.

And there was the little girl, lying in the middle of the road where no one seemed to travel. There was no one to take her in or to even throw a coin to her.

"Stop!" I cried, and I leapt out of the car as soon as I could to reach the girl. She was filthy, of course, but I pretended not to notice. I wanted to embrace her, but she shied away from me, so in lieu of human touch, I gave her my coat. It was a mild day, but she seemed to have a chill she couldn't shake. Next, I handed her the bag of pastries.

"Sweet girl," I said to her in French, and already I knew I had said the wrong thing. How did I know if she was sweet? She was only suffering.

She gave me a look of suspicion, but out of desperate need, she grabbed her first pastry. Apricot filling leaked from the corners of the pastry, and when I watched her eat, it felt as if I were putting food into my own mouth.

"Who are you? Why do you live here? Why do you appear in the mirror?"

There were no answers. She only ate faster, filling her mouth.

It's hard to convey how much time I spent waiting for her. She ate every pastry in the bag without thanking me or even really looking at me. How could she see me as a stranger? She'd spent so much time looking at me in the glass, pretending to eat my food with me.

"I'm safe," I told her. "I'm here to help you."

The bag of pastries did not refill itself by any magic. When she was done eating, I went to the driver and asked if the girl could come back to the house with us.

"There is room for only one," he said without looking me in the eyes. My captor played such funny games.

Before deciding what to do, I looked around to see if I could find the mirror that had linked my world and the girl's. But I couldn't find it anywhere.

If I had seen the mirror, if I could have seen my captor waiting for me on the other side, I might have made a different choice. As it was, I opened the car door.

"It is warm in here," I told the girl in French.

That was all she needed to hear. She ran to the vehicle, still wearing my coat.

"Are you sure?" the driver said.

"I am sure. Take her in my place."

I stepped back and watched the car drive away.

Maybe the girl was kept in that cold street by some spell. Whatever it was, I was immune to it. When the car left, I walked away, back to the main part of the desolate city. All I had in my purse was a train ticket back. I was afraid I would see the little girl and the driver when I went back to the train station. I knew the sight of them would hurt my pride, and I might start to cry. The day hadn't gone the way I had hoped.

Fortunately, they weren't there. Maybe they had already left, or maybe they were lingering in the city so the girl could have a hot meal and buy new clothes fit for her new place in a mansion.

On the train, I couldn't eat. My stomach ached. Now I was free. I didn't even know how long I had lived in the mansion. It must have been at least a year. Maybe more? I was so preoccupied, I barely enjoyed the dappled countryside rolling past me. Where would I go? The only place where I might be welcome was my old village, back at the house of my father.

When I reached my destination, no one was waiting for me on the platform of the train. I walked out of the city and into the woods. It was like I was a god because I wasn't tired or hungry, and I didn't feel like lying down. I walked and walked. Yes, perhaps my captor was a god and had made me like himself.

I knocked on my father's door. The old place was smaller than I remembered, and it had grown shabbier in my absence. No one had tended to the garden or painted the door when it faded. My father answered, and a smile lit up his face. For a minute, I felt like I was really at home again.

"I knew you'd find a way out!" he said, giving me a proud smile.

I nodded, unsure of what to say. Had I found a way out, or had my captor gotten rid of me? I had never been sure what he'd wanted from me. Maybe I'd disappointed him somehow.

"You must be starving," my father said, unbothered by my silence. "I was just about to go to the beer hall. They have a new dark beer that is really something special. And I'll buy you sausages and potatoes."

I shook my head. For the first time, I noticed how Bavarian he was. It was like I'd woken up from a dream, and I was trying to remember who I was.

"I'm tired now. You go on without me."

And so he did. Once he was gone, I examined my room to see if anything had been displaced, but nothing had changed except a thick layer of dust had gathered on all the surfaces. I got a rag and a broom and opened the window, and I began to make a clean space for myself again. And yet, there was something new! There was a long mirror almost hidden by my bed, affixed to my bare wall. There was not a speck of dust on the mirror's surface.

I felt dizzy as I looked in the glass. I was sure I'd see the little girl again, safe and warm in my old room at my captor's house. She'd be wearing my old clothes and eating her meals in front of the mirror, looking for me to join her. But no.

It was only me in the mirror. It was me and my old bedroom in my old village. I looked much older than I expected. It had been some time since I had looked into a mirror and seen myself.

When my father returned, I would tell him to take the glass away. He could pry it from the wall and sell it somewhere. I ignored my reflection as I bustled around, making my old room ready for myself again. Before I'd lived in my captor's house, I'd enjoyed the bustle of cleaning and the sight of a job well done. I'd had servants for so long, though. It had been so dreary in the mansion. So inexplicably and unutterably sad.

But I'd found a ransom for myself, hadn't I? The little girl had taken my place. Would my captor give her French lessons, or something else? I shuddered to think of what he might teach her.

So what, though? She'd find a way out. She would someday. And in the meantime, she'd be warm and fed. I'd helped her. I'd saved her life.

I had believed I could help my captor, too. I'd thought I could thaw something inside of him. Well, so what? Everyone fails at some endeavors.

I had a cup of tea, and I felt much better. I put on one of my old dresses, one I'd loved before going to the mansion. The fabric smelled musty, but it was comfortable.

It was night when I went outside. I didn't know where I was going. I had more strength and energy than I'd ever imagined. Maybe I could walk all the way to Paris. Or maybe I would wander over to the beer hall. I'd missed the heft of our local beer. My captor had always served me wine, which I had no taste for.

Maybe someone would be playing the accordion. Would I remember how to dance? I preferred dancing to talking. If my old friends asked me for my story, I would think of something better than the truth. Whatever my reasons, no one would blame me for leaving. Everyone from my village would have found the mansion ungodly, and they would have done everything the same as I did.

Glass Pet

My grandmother's kitchen was dark, and that was where she kept her dog. He whined all the time. He was made of glass.

I lived with my mother, but I never seemed to be at home. Maybe I was distracted when I was home, lost in a daydream, so I didn't notice where I was. Grandmother's house made me nervous, kept me on edge. I always knew where I was when I was there.

According to my mother and grandmother, a wolf lived in the woods outside my grandmother's house. I was as scared of the wolf as they were, but I planned to reason with him if I ever met him. I kept a pot of beans on the stove and a bag of fruit in the refrigerator, so I always had something to offer him.

My grandmother cared for her glass pet like he was her own arm, but she got so sick with fever, I had to take care of him.

Instead of eating food like a normal dog, he ate light. There weren't many lights in grandmother's house (she said they gave her a headache), but the dog had a special lamp, a very bright one. You knew he was eating if he got hot to the touch and glowed a little. I tried feeding him when my grandmother was too sick to get out of bed, but he refused to eat.

"Come on, little pup. I know you miss Grandma, but she's getting her strength back," I kept telling him. He whined like he always did, and he wouldn't fortify himself. He stayed cold as the glass on the windows that separated us from the winter night.

When I went to take Grandma her bowl of porridge, she wouldn't eat either.

"How is God?" That was what she called her pet.

"Pretty good," I said. I didn't want her to know he wasn't eating. I didn't want to seem incompetent. She always treated me like a kid, but I was brave enough to walk through the woods of ill repute to visit her. My mother wasn't nearly so brave.

"The wolf is tempting me," she said. "I'm afraid I'll succumb this time."

We stopped talking to listen to the cello playing outside her window. My grandmother always told me the wolf played the cello to tempt us to go outside. I had never seen the wolf. Whenever I tried to shine one of the lamps out the window, it didn't illuminate much of anything outside. It only helped me see my reflection more clearly.

"Don't go outside. It's cold out there," I said. I hoped that someday I would marry a man who could play the cello. Until then, the music helped me sleep, but I wasn't tempted to go outside and meet the one who played it.

"I could let him in here."

Was she serious? Her eyes looked eerie in the low light. I kept the lamp in the hall turned on, and it barely illuminated her bedroom when I opened her door. She didn't want any kind of light in her room. I wasn't sure what she did when she got bored. I kept a lamp in my room so I could read and knit.

"You're feverish. You aren't thinking clearly. You have to get better so you can see God," I said, and she began to cry. I left her alone. It was best to leave her when she was feeling repentant.

She always promised me that God would protect us from the wolf. I didn't know why she was so drawn to him.

I tried feeding the dog again, and again he refused, so I went to my room to occupy myself. I knitted a small blanket for the dog so he wouldn't get too cold while my grandmother was sick. I thought about using my skin to warm him, but whenever I brought him to my cheek, it was like caressing an ice cube. It made my cheek go numb.

My mother once told me that my grandmother couldn't afford a pet, but I didn't think the glass dog could be very expensive to maintain. We needed to keep some lights on anyway. And yet, if my mother hadn't sent food and medicine to my grandmother, and if I hadn't carried them through the woods, my grandmother would have died a long time ago. My mother wouldn't carry the supplies herself. She had always been so afraid of the wolf.

When I was finished composing my small blanket, I went to the kitchen so I could cover the dog.

"Sweet little pup!" I said as I put the gray blanket over its clear body. It whined, of course, but I was so used to it, it was like silence.

I glanced out the window to see if I could see the wolf. The cello music had stopped. Maybe he was resting, or maybe he was at one of our windows, watching.

I always stayed in my room at grandmother's if a visit ran long and lasted until after dark. Lately, it seemed it was always dark. But when the sun rose, I knew the wolf would go into his cave and he would rest. I just had to wait for the night to end.

As I prayed for the sun to rise, the dog stopped whining.

"What?" I said. I took the blanket off of his glass back, and I shook him. He was colder than death, and now he was silent.

I let out a scream. I begged the dog, and I prayed to God. "Don't die! Don't leave us alone! The wolf will get us!"

I shouldn't have carried on that way. I woke my grandmother, who started screaming. I heard her bed creak, and she padded into the hallway. I thought she was too sick to stand, but she ran at me and shoved me aside and took the dog up in her arms.

"Oh, God! God!" she called out. Then she turned to me. "Why didn't you tell me something was wrong?"

"What could you have done?" I said. "Pets don't live forever."

Her face was so white. Her lips, and even her eyes seemed white all the way through. She looked at me with a frozen face, a twisted gape of hatred. She had been so kind to me, and we had always shared what we had with each other. When she was younger, she would send food to my mother and me. It would have scared me less to see the wolf stare hungrily at me than to see my grandmother that way. It's much worse when someone you trust turns out to be ravenous.

The cello music started up again, so lovely and pleading.

My grandmother was very strong at that moment. I tried to overpower her, but she ran from me and unlocked the locks and flung open the door.

"Come in!" she shouted at the wolf. "It's all over. There's no protection for us anymore."

The music stopped. I grabbed the now-silent glass dog and ran back to my room. I locked the flimsy deadbolt and put a chair in front of the door and hid under the bed.

I could hear my pot of beans simmering on the stove. Why did I think I could stop the wolf from eating meat? My precautions were comforting lies I'd told myself. My mother had always warned me there was no way to outsmart the wolf.

While we were under my bed, I asked the dog, "Why did you have to die? Things were bad enough as it was."

It was pointless to ask him for protection now that he was dead. And yet. I thought I heard the slightest whine in his glass throat. I thought I heard some sign of life.

"Yes! Good dog, good!" I said.

Outside my bedroom, it was silent.

"Grandmother?" I called out.

She didn't answer. Instead, I heard the cello again. This time it was inside the house. Right outside my bedroom door.

I shook the glass dog. I held him tight. I pleaded with him. "Save me!"

The glass grew a little warmer, and I could hear a little whine again. He was still alive. Maybe he'd only been sleeping.

"He's alive again!" I shouted at the cello player. "He'll protect me!"

The music kept on. I began to cry. The glass dog was a little bit alive again, but he wasn't making the wolf go away. I waited under my bed curled in a ball, clutching the glass dog. If my grandmother had only waited patiently, held out hope that the dog would recover! If she had only waited until morning. She was sick, yes, and it made her weak, but had she learned nothing from the old stories?

Now that the wolf was in the house, time seemed to stop. Morning was not on its way. I grew hungry, and the music grew sweeter by the minute like a cake rising in the oven. I needed to go to the wolf. He was calling to me, and he was never going to go away. It was time, at long last.

I held the glass dog as a kind of lucky charm, and I unlocked my little lock (that a wolf could have easily torn off) and opened my door.

Outside in the hall, there was no cello. There was only a glass wolf. Inside his belly, my grandmother slept all curled up. She was smiling like she was having a wonderful dream. Was the wolf digesting, or was he gestating? I couldn't tell. I called out to my grandmother, but she couldn't hear me.

The music came from the wolf's throat. Now that I was in his presence, I could see that the pet we'd had so long was not a glass dog. He was a glass cub, the young offspring of this wolf. As he grew, his little whine would become a beautiful song. But we had taken him from his parent, from the strong nutrition that could make him grow. The wolf was full of light, and it was the cub's food. So close to the parent wolf now, the glass cub grew hot like a lightbulb left on all night. He burned my fingers, and without thinking, I dropped him on the hardwood floor.

He shattered. He was our friend, the pet we'd had so long. Now it was only me and the wolf.

The music stopped. The wolf grew silent and stared at the broken glass like he was trying to solve a complicated puzzle.

"I'm so sorry!" I said. "I didn't mean to hurt him! He was burning my hands. You made him too hot."

The wolf opened his mouth. The yawning glass made a sound like when you drop an ice cube into hot water. Inside the wolf's mouth, it was bright. The light in him was keeping my grandmother so warm and peaceful inside his belly, and he was so spacious. He bent down and swallowed up the broken pieces of the glass cub. When he was finished, I could see the glass pieces floating inside of him, and I knew they would find a way back together. The glass cub would live again.

The glass wolf kept his mouth open for me as an invitation. So polite. The lovely music resumed and leaked from his open maw. Why not go to be with my grandmother and our old pet? We'd all lived together so long. I had the feeling that whether I entered the mouth or ran back to my mother's house, my fate would be the same. I would end up in the wolf's belly eventually. I kept my eyes open as I stuck my head inside his mouth.

GLASS PIANO

I USED TO THINK I was the only one who had swallowed a glass piano. That was why I had to keep my secret, why I had to be so careful. I avoided the rough games that the other kids played when no one was looking.

The Glass Piano says: *I found you, and you found me. I give you my music, and you give me movement. I can go anywhere you go as long as you and I don't shatter.*

I blamed myself for so many years, until I told the family doctors. The terror of telling on myself kept me dyspeptic in my early years, baffling the experts. They tried different diets (all soft, a blessing), and they prescribed rest, and they gave me prayers.

By the time I told the doctors about the glass piano, I could have been a mother if I hadn't been so sick. A blessing. I could have been forced to do all sorts of things.

The doctors laughed when I said "As a child, I swallowed a glass piano."

I could feel the music building inside me, and I opened my mouth so they could hear. It was like I'd asked them to listen to the heartbeat of my doll. They put their ears near my mouth and murmured with such exaggerated frenzy, and they drowned out the little song. It's only the smallest tinkling song, and it's muffled by all my tissues.

When I sleep, the music fills my liver and kidneys and my rippling digestive trail. I thought I would die young.

The Glass Piano says: *I am so small, everyone swallows me.*

I remember the glass piano the way some recall their first love. The size of a coin, standing on delicate legs. I had everything then. I could have swallowed thousands of coins. I did.

Thank God I swallowed the piano and remembered it. Otherwise, I would have married a prince. They would have had me bear more princes. The piano would have shattered, and I would have died in my finery.

The Glass Piano says: *You are dying.*

I know I am.

The Glass Piano says: *I will find you in the afterlife. Listen for my song, the small sound muffled by the tissues of heaven.*

I left the palace and learned. I devoted my life to orphans. All because of the glass piano. In my religious life, the first orphan I met said she had a song stuck in her stomach, and opened her mouth, and I heard the brilliant tinkling. I laughed, delighted, and I told her about the glass piano. How wide her eyes were. How wonderful to pass on the fruits of your pain. From then on, she respected the glass piano inside her, though she couldn't remember swallowing it.

The Glass Piano says: *You had so many things, yet you only remember me.*

I've heard the music from so many mouths that now I know glass pianos are everywhere. I thought my fine life was my doom, that the others were happy because they'd never seen a glass piano shining like an eye in the candlelight. Who could resist such a thing? I had been playing rough games that morning before I swallowed the glass piano. I had eaten aged cheeses and nuts, foods that never passed my lips again for the rest of my life.

It was no different than swallowing a little lump of snow. A frozen soul. Later, I learned about cameras. Maybe that's what it was, a device to show God my insides.

The Glass Piano says: *My music was your resting place.*

Thank God I never had a normal life. I left the palace. I lived among the orphans. I am an orphan. I have lived.

(for Princess Alexandra of Bavaria)

Glass Mountain

During the day, the glass absorbed enough heat from the sun that the temperature almost felt like human flesh. If I took off my shoes, I could walk in a spiral around the top of the mountain without slipping, and that was a way to pass the time. Earth mountains towered over my glass mountain, and they were full of life. I watched an eagle hook small rodents to carry to a precarious nest for his eaglets. Eagles seem more like people than birds because they're large enough that you can see how terrible and loving they are.

That is to say, it wasn't so bad on Glass Mountain. At the very top of the mountain, it was flat instead of jagged, which meant I could lie down and sleep at night. The apple tree that grew at the top shed leaves for me to cushion and cover myself with, and it dropped more apples than I could eat.

I fell into a rhythm. I rested under the shade of the tree during the morning, walked in the afternoon, and ate apples constantly to stay hydrated and keep my spirits up. If I heard the painful thud of a body or any wailing below me, I looked up at the sky so I wouldn't have to see them. My father had warned me that many men wouldn't make it to the top of the mountain.

Every morning, my father shouted up at me from the bottom of the mountain to ask how I was doing. Obviously, I wasn't doing well. For weeks, I begged to come down, but he kept telling me, "This is the only way!" Eventually, I quit asking.

Once I gave up on leaving the mountain, I began asking my father if someone could bring me things like bread and wine and books and clean clothes. He always said, "Wait another day!"

I wore white hosiery that grew dirty, and my dress was embroidered with gold thread, which might have been impressive from a distance, but it soon felt sticky and stiff from dribbled apple juice. If I'd taken the dress off at night, I would have been too cold. For no particular reason I could find, my filthy feelings ended one day, and I stopped longing for a bath.

The man who made it to the top of my mountain would become my husband, and he would inherit my father's kingship. I got impatient, and one time I climbed down so I could teach the men how to climb properly, but my father yelled at me to go back to the top.

"I can help them!" I yelled back.

"You climb by magic. They must climb by skill!"

As if the country's future depended on a king who could climb glass.

I can't say how many weeks or months I was up there before I saw a man who seemed like he could make it. He was halfway up, and he had clever suction cups attached to his hands and feet. He had a beautiful smile. Even from far away, I could see the light in his eyes.

"Not him!" I whispered to myself. I didn't want him to die, but I couldn't imagine—I mean—forever. And the whole country would be his.

Before he reached the top, the suctions gave way. A look of fear, then desperation, then disbelief passed over his strong features. I should have looked away, but I watched him fall, and I heard the crack of his body hitting the glass at the foot of the mountain. He cried out in pain, and then he was silent.

"Why didn't I want him?" I asked myself. "It must have been my fault he fell."

I felt like a murderer. I made up a story for that climber who came the closest. I decided he had always been in love with me, observing me without my knowledge. These thoughts kept me awake at night. I started sleeping during the day so I didn't have to watch the climbers. I didn't want them to die for my sake.

One morning, I shouted down to my father, "Haven't you had enough? This contest is a punishment for me and your whole kingdom."

"Not yet," he said. "It's for the greater good!"

Some days, I dreamed I was king. I knew I would be a better king than my father. How many men in our country had died for the sake of his contest? I couldn't understand why he had done it, whether for entertainment or out of cruelty.

The one who finally pitied me was an eagle who flew to my side to see if I needed help. I wanted to stroke his mottled brown head, which looked so soft, but I was afraid I would chase him away. It had been a long time since I had touched anything that looked so soft.

"I can take you to my mountain," the eagle said.

But he smelled like death and garbage. He waddled closer to me. I'm sure I smelled awful, like fermented apples, but I'd grown used to my own smell.

"You could live in the nest until you're strong enough, and then you could live by the stream," the eagle said, having thought it over.

"I'm strong! I don't need help!" Could anyone survive on a glass mountain if they weren't strong? "Help one of those men below come to the top to get me. It's the only way to save the kingdom. Otherwise, who will reign when my father dies?"

The eagle looked sterner than usual. "You should refuse to play this game."

"But what about the kingdom?"

The eagle didn't understand. They don't have kingdoms. He felt he had to help me, though I wish he hadn't. Was it because I reminded him of an eaglet? Or maybe in spite of his protests, he knew he was like me. He had a part to play.

He swooped around and around the mountain, looking for a climber he could aid. I watched him settle on one who had slaughtered a bear and was using its claws to gain traction as he climbed. It was awful to see him use an animal's severed paws, but it must have impressed the eagle. The climber was strong and resourceful, just like the eagle was. So the eagle grabbed him with his talons and carried him to me.

I watched in excitement. I didn't care who won the contest anymore, who I would have to marry, who would rule. I only wanted my suspense to end.

The climber cried out in fear when the eagle lifted him. He didn't understand our plan. Instead of allowing himself to be flown into the air and set down by my side, the climber used his stolen claws to sever the eagle's talons.

In a flash, the climber fell towards me, tumbling into piles and piles of apple leaves and apple cores. The eagle's severed talons fell beside him. The eagle's body tumbled down the side of the mountain, and his corpse took its place among hundreds of men.

The climber was miraculously unharmed. He stood up and started to embrace me, but we both took a step back. He must have noticed how pungent I was, and I couldn't forgive him for what he had done to the eagle. He was clever, which was why he was destined to win, but he had climbed over corpses to get where he was, and he had slaughtered two animals. I hadn't realized it before, but I loved the eagle. I didn't know why, but I did. And I could never love this climber who'd made him bleed.

"You killed him!" I said. "He was trying to help you!"

The climber looked so confused. "I'm here to help you," he said, ignoring my strange grief over the eagle. "We've all been worried about you. We didn't know how you could survive up here."

Then I noticed that he was cut and bleeding, and he'd broken his arm, and he was limping. All for me and the kingdom.

I began to cry, but before I could say anything else, a band of servants rushed up the mountain to attend to me and my future husband. They carried us down on cushioned chairs, and they cleaned me, and my bathwater smelled like wine. They fixed me up and put me in a pink silk dress, but I couldn't stop crying. Everyone thought I was crying because I was so happy.

My father decided who could easily ascend Glass Mountain and who would have to struggle, but he never used his magic to prevent me from climbing down. He only used his warnings. If I had escaped or let the eagle carry me away, it would have saved so many.

There was nothing to do but wed the climber who cut off the feet of the eagle. I think the eagle was my best friend. I should have gone to live in a nest.

After our wedding, my father put a crown on my head and a crown on the climber's head. No one introduced me to the climber, and I didn't ask his name. After the crowning ceremony, my father gave me a dangerous smile. He said (like a child), "Watch this!"

He climbed to the top of Glass Mountain, and when he got to the top, he jumped. He joined all the corpses of the men who had died for his contest.

That was more than I could bear. I took off my crown and threw it at the feet of the climber who was my husband. Now that he was king, he could choose another queen. Before anyone could catch me, I ran. I took off my pink slippers so I could climb to the top of Glass Mountain. I'd been wrong about the eagle. The mountain was my best friend. At the top, I hugged the trunk of the tree, and I hungrily ate an apple. No other food had soiled my lips since I'd been rescued. I had believed I was uncomfortable up there, but it was the only place I could be myself.

"Come back!" My husband yelled at me from the bottom of the mountain.

In response, I threw down the eagle's severed talons. I told him, "I will return when you reattach the eagle's feet and bring him back to life."

He looked puzzled, but he promised me he'd do it.

I was the queen for the time being, and I'd created my own contest. Like my father's contest, it seemed impossible to win. I lived happily on the mountain while I waited, and I watched the strong eaglets leave their nest and teach themselves the deadly power of their talons.

Glass Pills

THE WOLF WAS jeweled with thorns, his belly slick with slime from the creek. Sick for decades. Spell thought she could rescue him from his deathlife in the murk.

"What happened to you?" was her first diagnostic question.

"Destiny." Due to his long teeth, he had to enunciate carefully.

"We could remove a few fangs," Spell said. She didn't mean to enrage him.

Fortunately, she had gauze and antiseptic at her house, where she worked for a charity that distributed glass pills.

"They purify your insides," she told the wolf. Of course, she also plucked the thorns and scrubbed away the slime, and he was grateful. She put a glass pill in his palm, and he held it up to the light.

"It doesn't glow," he said. "Must be plastic."

"The bottle says it's glass. It's probably not light enough outside."

Outside was sunset, red and gold. The pills were like bits of cloud.

"Have you taken one?" he asked her.

"No. I don't have the troubles they fix."

"You think you're so strong," he said.

"Healthy." She wanted to bite him.

"If you had seen what I've seen, lived the life I've lived, you wouldn't be so pristine."

"Clean," she whispered.

When they kissed, he dropped the glass pill on the floor, but it didn't shatter. Later, she picked it up and put it back in the bottle. The wolf left without taking any.

The next night, he broke the window of her bedroom and swallowed her whole.

Her cries were heard by a man who was chopping down trees in the middle of the night. He jumped through the broken window into her room and split the wolf's belly, pulled her free. Kissed her. She blushed, covered with goo. How could he love her that way?

"I'm brave," he said.

He had several tattoos, and she asked what they meant. Twelve white ribbons on his arms reminded him of dead friends. A smile on his neck reminded him of God. An ax on his hand reminded him that work would heal his sadness.

"Work doesn't heal anything," she said. When the time was right, she would tell him about the pills.

"We should clean this mess," he said, as if he hadn't understood what she said about work. She had hoped that if you saved someone's life, it would lead to true understanding.

"I need the wolf's body because I'm in love with you," she said.

"Loving me is foolish, but I'll accept it." He had a troubling cough. "But what does that have to do with the wolf?"

"To fully love you, I need one thing. You must crawl inside his belly, and I will sew you up. Then I will take the ax and rescue you."

He stared at the wolf, considering her plan.

"Is this some kind of feminist thing?" he said.

"I wish," she said.

When the man was inside the wolf and she had sewed him in, she kissed the wolf's cold and lipless mouth.

"Spell!" he cried out. "Help me!"

He played along well. She raised the ax, cut carefully, and saved him. So they were both covered in goo.

The next morning, they buried the wolf together. They repaired the broken window. They cleaned themselves.

"I'll show you where I live if you follow me," he said when they were finished with their chores.

She slipped a bottle of glass pills into her dress pocket and followed him deeper into the woods. His house was made of logs.

"Made it myself," he said. Sturdy enough.

"Good work."

He led her inside and showed her his handmade furniture. She sat on a chair and expected to get splinters, but he'd sanded it smooth. Everything he made had a lopsided beauty, an unexpected charm.

"How long have you lived here?" she said.

"Feels like a hundred years. I think I was asleep when I heard you scream."

"Sleeping while swinging an ax?"

"It's happened to other men."

There was only one room for his bed, his stove, his chairs. The room smelled like canned fish. A tall stack of newspapers filled one corner of the room.

"I'm trying to solve a mystery," he explained. "The papers are evidence. Otherwise, I'm a tidy man." He lit several red candles, which exhaled cinnamon breaths.

"I can help you solve your mystery if you'll help me solve mine," she said. "See, something is wrong with you. What is it?"

His phantoms might take any shape, but she remembered the glass pills in her pocket and felt safe.

"I'm fine," he said. "I built this house with my own hands. Maybe it's not as nice as yours, but who are you to scorn me?"

"It isn't the house," she said. "It's your pain. It's singed into your skin. The wolf's pain was foreign to me. Your pain is something I think I understand."

"I bet life was easy for you."

"My father is dead," she said.

"My whole family is dead."

"My father died in the war."

"My whole family died in the war."

"I saw him die in front of me."

"I saw them. In front of me. Blood and tears. Fire. I barely escaped."

"That is a bit worse than what happened to me," she said. It was hard to admit. She had suffered and been strong, committing her life to helping others. No glass pill had passed her lips because her life was glass enough. It was clean and clear, even if it didn't glow.

"I'm sorry to disappoint, but I need you to understand that you can never understand. Each person's pain is written in a different language," he said.

"But I know the translator. These are particles of God." She pulled the bottle from her pocket and gave it a rattle before putting it in his hands. "You've suffered enough."

"Glass pills?" He pulled one out. "Someone from your charity already gave me some. I've tried them. I think they're made of plastic."

Instead of grabbing his ax and chasing him (her first impulse), she cried instead.

"I'm sorry," he said. "I'll take the pills."

He took two, and they went to sleep. In the morning, she looked into his eyes and didn't know what he felt.

"I am a murderer," he said.

"You had to kill the wolf! He ate me! Doesn't my life mean anything?"

"I don't mean that," he said. "Something from before."

"Forget it. You'll feel better soon," she said.

He still believed work would heal him, so she let him chop down trees as long as he kept taking the bits of glass.

"Soon they'll make your stomach glow," she said, though they never caught the light. Perhaps there was a flaw in their design. And yet they'd saved so many people.

That night, she got back inside the wolf's belly, and he rescued her again. He climbed in next, and she rescued him. She hoped the game would never get old.

Glass Cabbage

THE OLD MAN and old woman were almost out of food. Salespeople sometimes took the path through the woods and dropped by their house to sell things like flour and oil and manufactured sweets, which supplemented their diet of eggs and vegetables and the occasional squirrel or rabbit. But their chickens and ripening vegetables had disappeared one night, and it had been weeks since a salesman from town had passed by.

"Maybe it was an animal who ate our vegetables," the old man said and they discussed the possibilities.

"Then who stole our chickens? A person must have stolen them. The pen's not damaged. There's no blood around."

The old man looked at the empty pen and wiped away a tear. "I reckon something bad has happened in town. It's what we've always predicted."

"But we don't smell smoke, and we haven't heard anything that sounds like disaster."

"It might have happened in a different way than we thought it would."

The woods were quieter than usual.

"I'll have to try again to find a squirrel," the old man said, though he hated to shoot them.

"I'll do some foraging," the old woman said, and they went their separate ways.

She made a final inspection of their vegetable garden for any overlooked scraps, and she found a wilting carrot top lying on the ground, so she tossed it into her sack. There had to be something deeper in the woods, some source of food. She was sure she'd die if she didn't find something soon.

Winter was threatening, and the birds had eaten all the berries. Under the tallest oak trees in the forest, she found a couple of mushrooms for her bag. Nothing else. She kept going until she was somewhere she didn't recognize. A thick row of thorn bushes seemed to have been placed specifically in her way, keeping her from something, so she pushed through them and ignored the pricks to her arms and face. On the other side, there was a field. A field! She didn't know there were any farmers in the middle of the woods.

"Don't get excited," she reminded herself. When things were bad, they usually got worse. Naturally, the field was plucked bare. Since she didn't notice anyone around, she decided to look to see if any bit of food was overlooked.

Inside a dug-up row, she found a tiny potato. Into the bag it went. Was that all? No, there was something else there, at the far end of the field. A beautiful large leaf hid (she knew) something ripe and edible. She ran to the thick leaf and lifted it like a veil, and underneath she found a hard thing that glinted in the afternoon sun. It was a huge cabbage made of green-tinted glass.

"A glass cabbage." She held it up to her face and whispered to it. Its surface was foggy with dew, but when she wiped it with her shirt, she saw something inside. A big toe. A rather large big toe.

She wished that the toe was a doll and that the toenail was the doll's face. It was hard to accept what it was. The severed bottom of the toe was neatly bandaged, at least, and the toenail was well-cared for. When she turned the glass cabbage, rolling it around to see the toe from different angles, the toe moved, too. It bumped against the glass edges in a way that looked painful. But there was no one to feel any pain from it, was there?

So freshly preserved, that toe was. Pale pink, like a healthy pig. Any piece of meat could be prepared. It would be like skinning a squirrel.

She couldn't fit the glass cabbage in her bag. It would have torn the seams. So she took up the cabbage in both arms and carried it home, needlessly shielding the glass from thorns. She couldn't stop staring at the big toe inside. It must have been the toe of a giant. Distracted, she didn't see a thick tangle of roots at her feet. She tripped, and the glass cabbage flew into the air. Before she could catch it, it fell on the hard roots and shattered.

She wanted to cry, but she stood up and picked her way through the broken glass to get to the toe. It was frightening to pick it up at first. And yet, she was desperate. She picked it up by its bandage and gave it a quick sniff. It had the same metallic smell as meat.

"It's a sign," she said to herself. She would have had to smash the glass cabbage to get at the big toe anyway. "Fresh meat."

She rushed along, feeling like she was in some kind of danger until she reached her backyard. There, she prepared the toe. She half-ignored what she was doing, knowing she couldn't relish her meal as much if she thought about the discarded parts. This was even easier than a squirrel in one sense. No guts. She used her ax to remove the toenail, and she peeled away the bandage, and she tried not to look at the toe before she dropped it in her boiling pot of water. She quickly dug a hole to bury the toenail and the bandage.

She put the measly carrot top and mushrooms and the tiny potato that she'd found into the pot, and she used some salt from her cupboard. After some time, the smell was intoxicating, and she looked into the pot and saw that the skin was beginning to separate from the meat. She pulled it off with metal tongs and dug a quick hole to bury the skin. She hated to waste any part of the meat, but there was something disturbing about that skin. It had the faded labyrinth of a toe print on it. Had it been another animal's skin, she would have eaten it.

When the thing was cooked, it looked so tender. She used her tongs to shred the meat, and finally, she removed the bone from the stew and put it into another hole she'd dug. Soon, the remnants of the toe were buried in three different spots in her yard, and she had a delicious stew in her pot. She used her ladle to give it a taste, and it tasted no different from pork stew. Maybe it was even better.

She kept tasting, waiting for the old man to return. If the stew kept cooking, the meat would get tough. Finally, she decided to ladle herself a bowlful.

He was far away, no doubt, trying to set a slow trap for some creature. It was annoying of him not to know when to give up.

As she was eating the stew, she was disturbed a time or two by memories of finding the big toe and preparing it for the pot. It made her shiver to remember what it had been. Thinking about the buried remnants upset her, too. It was like she'd killed a man and buried his corpse in her yard.

No, no, it was nothing to worry about. If anything, the toe was meant for her. It had been placed there in that glass cabbage (which must have been some kind of magic), and it was like it had called her name. She had known just where to go to find it.

When was the last time she had eaten so well? Maybe years. The salesmen were willing to trade with them, to accept eggs for their goods, but the old woman suspected they were taking pity on them. When she was hungry, she hadn't cared, but now that she was almost full, she was beginning to feel ashamed. Anyone who lived in town must have found them awfully pitiful. Maybe the old man liked being an object of pity because it made him interesting, and he liked to talk to the salesmen who wandered by and tell them stories of life in the woods, but the old woman didn't like it. She saw herself as strong and happy, and the old man seemed to see her that way too. It confused her when others didn't see her the same way, and it made her ask herself unhelpful questions. What was so great about being from one of the towns?

She kept eating. Her stomach raged for it, for every drop of it. When she was finished, she even used her fingers to scoop out the bits of carrot top stuck to the walls of the pot, and she savored the bits of grease that clung to the greens.

While she ate, she kept thinking the old man would catch her red-handed. But he didn't. By the time he came home, it was pure night, and the pot had already been scrubbed and the fire put out. She was in bed when she heard him open the door. She pretended to be asleep when he came into the bedroom and took off his clothes and lay down beside her.

"I can smell it outside. You found something. You didn't wait for me," he said.

"What do you think about that?" she said without opening her eyes.

"I was trying too hard to find what wasn't there. But you still should have saved me something. Some scrap of something." He didn't sound angry or even sad. He sounded like his feelings had floated away, up into the night sky.

"I did it for a reason, but I don't know what the reason is," she said. "I was so hungry. I think my body knows something."

"You want me to die?" he said.

"No. I just want to live."

The toe was meant for her. It thundered in her body as she digested it. It might have been an evil toe. But it was hers. The old man might have gotten sick when he realized what he was eating. He might have ruined the meal.

They couldn't make sense of it, either together or separately. Without meaning to, the old woman fell asleep. Some time later, a voice in the distance woke her up.

"Who?" That was all she heard at first. "Who?"

"It's someone from the town," she said to herself. "They're having a disaster. But I'm not going out there."

The voice was still distant, but it seemed to draw closer. "Who? Who? Who stole?"

"I didn't steal," she said aloud, sitting up in bed. The old man was snoring beside her.

"Who stole my big toe?" The voice was like a whistling wind prefiguring a tornado or terrible hail.

"I didn't steal it! You left it there!"

In spite of her protesting, she found herself running through the darkness to look outside for the source of the voice. The night was clear and cold. It must have been a bad dream.

No, there it was again. "Who stole?" It was as if a person had merged with a cloud or the moon and tried to speak through it. Whatever it was, the creature was getting closer.

"Show yourself!" she shouted. "If you're going to accuse me, then do it to my face. I won't be afraid of a possibility. You set me up to fail. I was hungry, and you put your toe out there, and you expected me not to eat it? It was calling to me!"

"You stole my big toe!" the voice said, but it was quieter than before.

"The choice you gave me wasn't fair." She felt ashamed for her complaints, like she was a child whining to her parents. But this was life or death. It was the difference between guilt or innocence.

She waited for the voice to accuse her again, but it didn't.

Glass House

MY HOUSE DECIDED it was time to go underground. I made the birds and beasts jealous by living in a nest of the shrugged-off skins of angels. Maybe angels were jealous of me, too. But no one wants to live like me.

In their ignorance, people want to live within layers of marble and gold. They miss being fetal, so they curl up and cover themselves in opaque shells.

But I want to see through, even now. Through my glass walls, I see packed earth and roots and curling worms. Through the soil, the breaths come: breaths of hot winds fog my walls, and breaths of ice leave tributaries of frost.

I conjure my own sun in the kitchen to warm my cheeks while I knead dough. I make gray clouds cluster over my chair as I write verses. If my glass house never rises, and if no one ever finds me, I will send my verses into people's dreams, and they will wake up singing about me.

The old druids who went before me became trees that can never be cut. They keep old wisdom in their sleeping core while their branches and roots receive news of the world. But they cannot read.

I have thousands of books (scribbled on the scabs of trees), some in dead languages I am resurrecting. I dream, but I never sleep.

In my dreams, I am a wren. Like him, I was once ruler of winter and ruler of the hedge. When I look at a tree, I can see into its heartwood where it keeps the marks of every season. As a wren, I visit my old friends.

The king and queen are dead in tombs of gold and marble. My old students are buried in humbler materials, and they are dissolving into dirt. They are lucky.

My only living friends are the trees. I nest in their branches, and through my feathers, I can feel the real sun and rain. My nest is protected by lightning. If you reach in to harm me, it will be your end.

This is not a glass prison, but if it were, I am free in my dreams. This is not a tomb, but if it were, I would be safe. This house is sacred and hard. Once it showed me the beauty of the river and the trees and sky, and now it shows me the beauty of the loamy dark.

GLASS APPLE

THE GLASS APPLE was a wedding present given by a stranger. He wore a monk's cloak, but Nix suspected he wasn't really a man of God.

"This is a gift from God, and God said not to eat it," the monk told her as he handed her the cool burden. It was small and asymmetrical, more like a wild crabapple than something from her husband's orchard.

The last thing she wanted to do was eat glass, whatever it was shaped like. It would slice her gums and turn her mouth into a bloody gruel. That kind of wound would soon rot and kill her. And she didn't even like ordinary apples, having had a bad experience once or twice. She couldn't believe the glass apple was a present from God. Wasn't God supposed to know her through and through, better than she knew herself?

She had received many blessings, though, and surely they were from God. The glass apple was given to her at midnight after her luckiest day when she'd found both love and vengeance.

"Why would God give me this?" she asked the monk, bowing her head and hoping she seemed grateful.

They stood in partial darkness, in a grove of trees a short distance from the torches and fiddling of the party. She had gone there to get away from the noise so she could think. So much had happened to her, and she wondered what she had done to deserve it all. Some people loved her and some hated her, but it was all so fierce. She had never felt as strongly about anything as people seemed to feel about her.

"God is a mystery even to me," the monk said. "But since it is a fruit, however rarified, I expect it contains some seeds."

The monk's fishy eyes glowed like two moons. The glass apple was a third moon that she held in her hands.

She tried to look deep inside to find the seeds, but it was hard to see. Light bounced around within the thing, forming walls of light. She brought it close to her left eye and shut her right and got lost in its depths. The seeds were hidden somewhere behind the shimmering (if the monk was indeed a monk and one who told the truth).

When she looked up, she saw that the monk had walked away, and she heard her new husband calling her name.

She received many presents after the wedding, but nothing held her attention as much as the glass apple, which she always kept near her. Somehow, she managed to hide it from her new husband and his servants and all the others who surrounded her in her new station. That was the first miracle. No one else seemed to see the apple. She hid it underwater during her bath and beneath her mattress when she slept and behind her husband's back while he kissed her. Her doubts about the apple faded. Gifts from God were always lucky.

She had already been lucky, but she needed more luck. It was hard to sleep and breathe and eat. So much had happened to her. And she was afraid the luck of the glass apple was the promise of children or more wealth, which she didn't need.

Her husband had two children, two boys, from a previous marriage. His wife had died while carrying the third. Nix's mother had also died when she was young, so she felt sorry for the children. She rarely saw them, though. They were brought in at dinner with combed hair and practiced smiles. Her husband and his friends did all the talking at dinner, so she didn't get to know the children. Maybe she could have visited their rooms to comfort them, to reassure them that their mother still loved them wherever she was, in that land where dead mothers went. Nix began to believe that deadland was where the glass apple had been born.

She stayed in her room as much as possible so she could be close to the glass apple. At night while her husband slept, she whispered into the glass apple, as if it had a hole for an ear.

"Please grant me courage," she told the apple. Sometimes she confessed to it, "I miss you."

Each day at dawn, after her husband left their bed and before the servant arrived, she brought the glass apple out from beneath her mattress and tried to see the seeds inside.

"Help me see the seeds," she asked the apple. It was the only clue the monk had given her. She looked inside so many times, she should have found something. Even if the seeds were glass seeds, the outlines should have been visible at certain angles. But in spite of being translucent, the glass was so attacked by light and somehow thick at its very core, she couldn't find anything inside.

And then she did see something. It was a year after her wedding, the night she'd received the apple. She wanted to believe it was exactly a year after receiving it, though in truth, it was more like a year and a month. That morning, the dawn was obscured by gray and fog, nothing rosy-cheeked about it. Maybe that morning, less light was there to cloud the center of the apple.

When she looked inside, she was shown a tiny picture that appeared to move. Nix saw her young self in crisis, her late stepmother beating her with a wooden doll. Somehow Nix had forgotten that memory. The old woman was dead, after all, so what point was there in reliving old slights?

The sight filled her with a chill, and she hid the glass apple under her mattress. She left it alone for the rest of the day as she worked on plans for a birthday celebration for her husband's eldest son.

The next morning, she was nervous as she looked into the glass apple. When it was impenetrable, it had been her friend, but now she was afraid of it. This time, the apple showed her a picture of her stepmother writhing in pain.

She began to think the glass apple was poisonous. It must have been a trick, a gift from an old enemy.

Still, she looked inside every morning, and every morning she received a fresh wound. She grew so haggard, her husband insisted that she stay in bed. That gave her more time alone with the glass apple. The apple began to show her unspeakable things, things she was sure had never happened.

Her sleep was haunted. Awake, her heart burned like someone had touched it with a hot iron.

A search for the monk who'd given her the gift was fruitless. She sent her servants to ask around at the local monasteries for a monk with wide eyes who'd once owned a glass apple, but they always returned with no answers. Everyone was very careful around her, always positive and kind. They treated her the way she'd treated her own sick mother, with awe and pity. As if the dying are the only ones who ever die.

She stopped asking the apple for help, but she couldn't stop looking. She saw a man with a knife. Ashes. A locked door. Blood on the floor. Bulbous sores. Phantoms of the past and future. Worst of all, she saw a nothing place. What if the souls of dead mothers went nowhere?

There was only one solution, the way she saw it. The glass apple had to disappear. The only way to rid herself of the glass apple was to eat it. She had to eat it. She imagined it many times. If she broke her teeth on the first try, she could smash the thing and grind it with her shoe heel and mix the pieces in her porridge. It had to go inside her. There was no other place for the thing.

One day, she ventured a taste of the apple. She put her tongue to the glass.

It was delicious. It wasn't like any apple she had tasted before, though. It was neither tart nor sickly sweet. It was more like a peeled pear, wholesome as something stolen.

She ventured the smallest bite, a gentle nibble. It gave beneath the pressure of her teeth, and a tiny chunk of it dislodged into her mouth. When she crunched it between her teeth, it didn't hurt. A burst of juice tickled her tongue, and the flesh gave way to chewing.

When she examined the apple, it still appeared to be glass, but a little piece was missing. That piece was inside her, sugar in her stomach.

She could still see a picture inside the thing, a picture of her mother taking her last breath. But it wasn't so clear anymore.

Another lick. Another bite. It didn't burn her stomach. It was a balm. The second bite was sweeter than an apple or a pear. It was a cherry. The third bite was honey. It would be selfish to keep it to herself. She had to share it.

She called in an old servant and asked her to take a bite. The woman gave Nix that hollow look of pity that the living give the dying, but she couldn't refuse. The servant put her lips to the object, and her eyes lit up. She sucked on it, and Nix laughed. It was juice in the other woman's mouth, too.

Her stepsons were called in, and then her husband, and then the local priest. It was a miracle, they all declared. Nix had received a miracle.

In all, she shared the transformation of glass to fruit with six others. She reserved the final bite for herself, but first she looked inside it. The picture was hard to see, so she squinted. She saw a picture of herself all curled up in a fetal position, planted in the ground like a seed. The picture moved, and she was a fruit tree, each blossom producing a new self.

The last bite was sweet as blood. It warmed her stomach, and her mind was filled with pictures. One self ran away to live in the forest all alone. Another self found old friends. Another self made new ones. Another self died and went to the glass world where all the souls of dead mothers collected like beads of dew on uncut lawns.

The self that remained at home was changed. Everyone was afraid of her because she glowed like the moon, and like the moon, she hid the souls of the dead inside her glass womb. No one could truly see inside of her because the light was never right. She still had enemies who wanted to destroy her, but she would have shattered their teeth if they had tried. She lived out the rest of her days in peace, waiting for the blissful day when God would chew her up and relish every bite.

Acknowledgments

Glass Tower – original to this collection
Glass Mother – original to this collection
Glass Book – first published in *ergot.*
Glass Pet – first published in *Seize the Press*
Glass House – first published in *Tales from Between*
Glass Clue – first published in *Cosmic Horror Monthly*
Glass Art – original to this collection
Glass Coffins – (or "The Wrong Mall") first published in the anthology *Monstrous Futures*
Glass Museum – original to this collection
Glass Angel – original to this collection
Looking Glass – original to this collection
Glass Turtle – original to this collection
Glass Piano – first published in *hex*
Glass Mountain – first published in *Interzone Digital*
Glass Pills – original to this collection
Glass Cabbage – first published in *Tales from Between*
Glass Apple – first published in *Magazine of Fantasy & Science Fiction*

I appreciate all the help I've received with these stories. Many people read, encouraged, and made suggestions to the stories in this collection, including (but not limited to) Seán Padraic Birnie, Samuel Moss, Matthew Stott, Rebecca Summerling, Christi Nogle, Katie McIvor, Sheree Renée Thomas, NM Whitley, TJ Price, Erik McHatton, Tim Bloom, JAW McCarthy, Ken Hueler, Gareth Jelley, Daniel Miller, Charles Tyra, Carson Winter, Zachary Gillan, Alex Woodroe, Kelsea Yu, Jonny Pickering, Brennie Shoup, Karlo Yeager Rodriguez, Rebecca Harrison, and others.

A version of the story from "Glass Cabbage" was told by my Grandfather Grimes.

This book wouldn't be here without Jon Padgett, whose fiction is an inspiration, and who takes chances on new writers.

Thanks to my parents, Stephen and Carol, and my brothers, Sam and Ben. Thanks to my husband, Justin, for everything.

Thanks to my friends for the encouragement. Thanks to my enemies for the inspiration. Thanks to God for the memories.

ABOUT THE AUTHOR

Ivy Grimes was born in Alabama and currently lives in Virginia. She is very quiet and enjoys puzzles. Her stories have appeared in *Vastarien*, *Interzone*, the *Magazine of Fantasy & Science Fiction*, *hex*, *ergot.*, *Seize the Press*, and elsewhere. Also available are a chapbook of short stories called *Grime Time* and a novella called *Star Shapes*. Visit her at www.ivyivyivyivy.com.

www.ingramcontent.com/pod-product-compliance
Lightning Source LLC
LaVergne TN
LVHW092050060526
838201LV00047B/1317